The Hangdog Hustle

a Nell Fury mystery

The Hangdog Hustle

a Nell Fury mystery

by
Elizabeth Pincus

Spinsters Ink
Duluth

First edition.
10-9-8-7-6-5-4-3-2

Spinsters Ink
32 E. First St., #330
Duluth, MN 55802-2002

This is a work of fiction. Any similarity to persons living or dead is
a coincidence.

"Homeless" by Jenifer McKitrick, ©copyright 1992
by Jenifer McKitrick. Used by permission. All rights reserved.

Cover art and design by Lois Stanfield, LightSource Images

Production by:

Lindy Askelin	Lou Ann Matossian
Melanie Cockrell	Jami Snyder
Patty Delaney	Jean Sramek
Helen Dooley	Liz Tufte
Joan Drury	Susan Vaughan
Kelly Kager	Lee Ann Villella
Carolyn Law	Nancy Walker

Library of Congress Cataloging-in-Publication Data

Pincus, Elizabeth, 1957–
      The hangdog hustle : a Nell Fury mystery / by Elizabeth Pincus.
1st ed.
            p.   cm.
      ISBN 1-883523-05-2 : $9.95
      I. Title.
PS3566.I517H36   1995
813' .54–dc20   94-37956
                                                                        CIP

Printed in the U.S.A. on elemental chlorine-free paper

For Elizabeth C.

Elizabeth Pincus is the author of two previous Nell Fury novels, *The Solitary Twist* and the Lambda Award-winning *The Two-Bit Tango*. She is the film critic for *Harper's Bazaar* magazine, and a frequent contributor to a number of other publications, including the *LA Weekly*, the *San Francisco Chronicle* and *Gay Community News*. Pincus, an ex-private eye, is currently at work on her fourth Nell Fury novel.

1

I was dragging a cardboard file box across the scarred wooden threshold when the elevator down the hall thudded to a halt. The doors trundled open. I glanced up to see a fellow in a bowler hat step cautiously into the corridor and aim his cane in my direction.

I finished pulling the box inside, then peered around the doorjamb. Yup, he was still heading my way, meandering down the length of the hallway like an inchworm in steady pursuit of its supper.

I whipped my new eyeglasses out of my shirt pocket. They were a soft tortoiseshell brown that matched my eyes and made me feel sexy and competent, like I ought to be trading banter in a newsroom with Rosalind Russell. Instead I was on my own, setting up a private eye office in the Tenderloin. Oh, well. It suited me. And from the looks of things, I even had a client on the way to help me christen the new digs.

I stepped back into the hall. The guy in the bowler had made some progress. I walked forward to greet him, then felt a hollow ache take hold in the vicinity of my heart. This was no old man. Thanks to my prescription lenses, I realized he was a guy maybe a decade older than I was, hobbled prematurely by disease.

I made myself smile. I pulled up beside him and said, "Can I help you?"

Bowler Hat squinted at me, causing his eyes to disappear like the retracting headlights of a sports car. His crow's feet were perfectly symmetrical, two tiny fans framing a kindly face. My heartache kicked up a notch.

"Yes, please," he said. "I'm looking for a woman named Nell Fury."

Bingo. I reached for his hand and gave it a gentle pump. "That's me."

"My dear, you're so young." His squint deepened.

"You were expecting, what, Miss Marple?"

Bowler Hat chuckled. "Lord, no! But Dave Brandstetter, perhaps, a female version."

I grinned. "Well, you got it half right. Come on in."

I cocked my head towards the office door and gestured him inside.

My new office was a big sunny rectangle on the fifth floor of a building on Taylor Street. It must have been a swanky place in the early half of the century, with its marble entranceway, shiny wood detailing, and the once-posh Golden Gate Theatre next door. I could practically smell the cigar smoke and cologne of a bygone era. Now, 25 Taylor was a little on the seedy side. The big, money outfits had moved up the street to San Francisco's sleek financial district, leaving Tenderloin office space for social service agencies, non-profits, and low-rent operatives like me.

"How long have you been a private investigator?" Bowler Hat was looking quizzically at the pile of boxes cluttering the floor of the office.

"Um, six, seven years," I replied, walking over to open the blinds. When I pulled the cord, bits of grime showered down from the yellowed slats. Rats. I should've cleaned before I moved in all my stuff.

I explained that I'd just switched offices, from an industrial warehouse space near China Basin to this building in the heart of the city. The new office reminded me of the first place I'd worked as a p.i., the Continent West Detective Agency down on Market Street. I told my prospective client I'd apprenticed there for three years, and had been solo now for almost four.

"Good," he said slowly. "So you know. . .people?"

"I get around." I planted a fist on my hip and looked at him sideways. "I bet you have a name."

He nodded his head in an almost courtly bow, both hands resting lightly on the handle of his cane. "Bartholomew Lane. Friends call me Laney." His pale lips curled upward. "That extends to you."

"Laney," I said.

My eyes started misting up. Damn. My friend Zeke had died three months ago and I was still smarting over that. Another friend recently found out she was HIV-positive and yet another had lost a lover just last week.

I was making a big assumption about Bartholomew Lane, but somehow I knew I was right. My typewriter, file folders, pens, and other office paraphernalia were littering the available chairs. I pulled off my glasses and did a quick swipe of both eyes, then hoisted the old Royal onto the window ledge, transferred other items to the desk, and gave Laney his choice of seats. He settled on the wooden swivel chair, rotating slightly until the midday sun fell across his chest in hazy diagonal stripes. I plopped into my magenta leather easy chair, leaned forward, and asked, "What can I do for you, Laney?"

He reached bony fingers into his suit jacket and extracted a smudged envelope. Lifting the flap, he shook out a sheaf of newspaper clippings. One of them floated to the floor, nestling among the dust clouds under the corner of the desk. I scooted over to snatch it, then straightened slowly as I gazed into a familiar face captured in grainy black and white.

Laney said, "That was his high school graduation picture. But he didn't look much older than that when he died."

I nodded.

"You know the story, Nell?"

"It's ringing a bell."

"He lived in my building. In the Castro, up on Diamond Street. We were . . . acquainted . . . ."

I studied the photo as Bartholomew Lane gave me a recap of Kent Kishida's murder. A couple of months ago, Kishida's ravaged body had been found near a side street up the hill from the Castro. He had been partly obscured by bushes when some neighborhood kids tripped over him; his back was ragged with stab wounds, his wallet missing. The assailant—or assailants—had never been apprehended. Technically, the case was still open, but Homicide had come up dry in the hunt for suspects.

Kent could have been the victim of a random mugging, a personal quarrel, a racist assault, or a gay-bashing. Or some combination of the above. No one knew for sure. Almost no one, that is.

I blew some dust off the clipping. Kishida wore oval wire-rim glasses and a delicate chain around his neck. He was smiling, just barely. A mole the size of a teardrop hung high on his left cheekbone. I shook my head and waited for the sudden wail of fire engines on Market Street to subside.

"I remember now. This happened the same week that other guy—"

4

"That's right!" Laney interrupted, jerking forward abruptly. His entire collection of clippings spilled to the floor.

I scrambled to retrieve them and dumped the whole pile on my desk. "The other guy—he's still in the news. What's his name? Schindler?"

"Uh-huh. Allen Schindler."

"Oh, yeah."

"Schindler was killed because he was gay, no question about it, but Kent—" Laney turned his palms to the ceiling. "Who knows?"

Schindler was a sailor in the U.S. Navy who was beaten to death by a couple of shipmates. It happened offshore at a naval base in Japan. The Navy initially tried to paint it as a barroom brawl, but after intense scrutiny, the true motive for the attack became evident. Schindler's murder—and the whole issue of homophobia in the military—became headline news.

Laney reminded me that Kent Kishida's body had been found just days before Schindler's death. Though initially newsworthy, Kishida's name soon faded from the spotlight when there was no progress in the case. The police never found his wallet or the murder weapon. And they still had no suspects.

Allen Schindler remained a cause célèbre, but Kent Kishida had become just another sorry statistic.

I unfolded my legs and rested a heel on the window sill. Bartholomew Lane tipped back his bowler, revealing a sparse fringe of yellow hair, fine as corn silk and damp with sweat. A bank of clouds had moved across the winter sky, but even without sunlight the office was a trifle warm. As if on cue, the old steam radiator in the corner started kicking up a fuss.

I planted my oxfords on the floor and asked, "Were you and Kent lovers, Mr. Lane?"

"Lord, no, only in my dreams!" He torqued his neck from left to right. "We were friends, though. He'd been a tenant in my building for a number of years. I'm the apartment manager."

"Ah, I see." I let a beat go by. "You still haven't told me why you're here."

Faint smile. "I know, dear, I'm sorry, I'm taking too much time." The smile faded. "I want to hire you. To find out what Kent was up to when he died."

"What do you mean, 'what he was up to'?"

"Kent was a young man, a bit of a party boy. He had a good job, too—he worked maintenance out at the Presidio. But he never seemed too concerned about, um, politics or anything, you know?"

"Mm-hmm."

"Then this summer, he started keeping longer hours. Going to the library. Meetings. I didn't think much of it, just that he'd found a career interest or something. But after he was killed—" Laney arched an eyebrow, then reached up to wipe a folded bandanna across his temple. The tendons on the back of his hand stood out like the fallen twigs of a winter oak.

"You think there's a connection?" I asked.

"I didn't at first. But Kent's mother called me a few days ago . . ."

I propped both feet on the window ledge and kept one eye on the horizon while Laney spoke.

Half an hour later I was scouring every exposed surface with Murphy's Oil Soap and mulling over Laney's story. The rest of it went like this: Kent's mother, Carmelinda Kishida, lived in the small farming town of Watsonville, just south of Santa Cruz. She and Kent had not been close, but after the funeral, she'd been the one to clean out his apartment. Kent's father was dead; he had no siblings or other relatives living nearby. So Carmelinda had hauled away Kent's few possessions in a borrowed pickup truck.

She had shown little interest in the police investigation. And that's the last Laney had seen or heard from her.

Until this Monday. She'd called, panicky, and ordered Bartholomew Lane to leave well enough alone. She kept screaming that the past was past—that Lane should mind his own business. He didn't know what she was talking about. Before hanging up, she uttered, "I've burned everything, anyway!"

Laney tried calling her back, but Carmelinda never answered the phone. He spoke with a few of the tenants in the apartment building, and no one knew what to make of it. He even called the cops. The inspector in charge of the Kishida investigation had dismissed Kent's mother as a nut case. Finally, Laney relayed the story to a gathering of friends, including Barney, a bartender at a neighborhood watering hole called The Mint.

As fate would have it, Barney and I went way back—I'd been a regular at the Mint for years. Barney had told Bartholomew Lane to look me up. Laney had consented, figuring a private eye might help ease his mind.

I wasn't so sure about that, but I told Laney I'd take the case. For two hundred dollars a day plus expenses, I agreed to poke into Kishida's last few months. So here I was—in the waning hours of another fretful year—with a messy office, a solemn heart, and a whole new load of trouble to call my own.

2

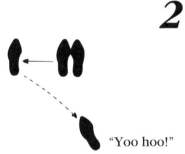

"Yoo hoo!"

I sat back on my heels and looked over my shoulder. Had I heard that right? Yoo hoo?!

"Yoo hoo! Hu-llllooo!"

I stood up too quickly, bashing my shin against the edge of a metal file drawer. I winced and bit my lip to keep from cursing.

"Oh, phooey, look what I made you do!" Heels clicked across the tile floor. "Are you all right, honey?"

I grinned crookedly. "Sure, sure."

The woman bearing down on me was a buxom gal, at least 5'10", and improbably tan for December in San Francisco. She wore spike-heeled sandals with red patent-leather bands across the toes, a cinched-waist dress, and blue-black curls caught high in a red velvet bow. Hmm—Barbie, by way of Miami Beach.

I dangled my foot back and forth to shake out the pain, then extended a hand. Barbie gave it a hearty workout and bellowed, "Welcome to the fifth floor!"

"Ohhhh." Phew, I thought she was another client. "You work here?"

"Right next door, honey. I'm in talent. What do *you* do?"

She gave it a lascivious lilt, casting an eye laden with blue shadow around the office that was finally achieving a semblance of order. I'd cleaned, swept, and stashed everything in its appropriate drawer. I was feeling mighty pleased with my bare furnishings: beat-up mahogany desk set, magenta chair, canary-yellow filing cabinet. The latter was an office-warming gift from my best friend Phoebe and her main squeeze, Johnnie Blue.

I said, "I'm a private detective."

"Shut my mouth!"

"Truly." I couldn't help but smile.

Barbie was dumbstruck. Slowly, a throaty growl rose up from her impressive chest. "Ha! *Perrrr*-fect. Let's drink to that!"

"Uhhh . . ."

"What's wrong? You still workin', honey?" She glanced at her wrist. "It's after five. And it's New Year's Eve! I bet you've got a bottle in that desk . . . ."

"Well, uhhh, I—"

Barbie cut in with a dismissive wave. "Hey, listen, I'm sorry. I come on kinda strong. What'd you say your name was?"

"I didn't. Nell. Nell Fury."

"Pleased to meetcha. I'm Merle. That's M–E–R–L–E, as in Haggard, not Streep." She showed me a pair of dimples. "Rain check, okay?"

Suddenly she was bustling over to the window, cracking

the blinds with two shiny red fingernails. The streetlights were just coming on. In the dim twilight glow, her skin was the color of flame. "Same view as mine." She whirled and surveyed the room one more time. "Nice place. But you need a plant or something."

"Uh, I—"

Merle didn't let me get a word in.

"That's okay, Nell. I'll handle it. I'm *on the case*." She winked and was out the door.

I listened to the cacaphony of heel taps move down the corridor. Jesus.

I was bending over to examine my damaged shin when the telephone trilled. Hey, cool. I didn't know my new lines were hooked up. I snagged it on the second ring. "Fury Investigations."

"Nellie. How's that file cabinet?"

"An eyesore." I smiled into the phone. "I love it."

"All right. Are you coming over later?"

"Yup."

Phoebe Grahame and Johnnie were living together now, in a tony townhouse at the top of Twin Peaks. Johnnie Blue, a stand-up comedian, was finally making some bucks—she'd done an HBO special and a stint on MTV. Next, she was slated to appear on Letterman. I'd promised to come over at midnight to toast their good fortune. And the new year, of course.

"Phoebes, I've got a new case."

"Oh yeah?"

"Yeah, remember Kent Kishida? That guy who was killed, back in October?"

"Ummm, I think so . . . ."

"I'm looking into it."

"Isn't that S.F.P.D. territory?"

"Well, they've sort of thrown in the towel." Phoebe was right, though; I don't normally mess with homicide. I continued, "I'm mostly gonna do some background work. Maybe zero in on a motive."

"Who's the client?"

"This guy. The building manager where Kishida lived."

"What's his interest?" I could practically feel Phoebe's skepticism vibrating through the telephone wire.

"They were friends." I didn't add that Bartholomew Lane desperately wanted to clear up the mystery before he died. He'd finally explained that to me as he was leaving the office.

"Watch your step on this one," Phoebe said.

"Sure thing."

"See you later, sweetheart."

"See ya."

We rang off. I lifted the first aid kit from my bottom desk drawer and cleaned my scraped shin, plastering a Betty Boop Band-Aid, the only kind I had, over the tender spot. I shook my head and eyeballed the jagged tear in my pants leg. Another pair of cut-offs in the making.

Replacing the first-aid supplies, I accidentally jostled something tucked in the back of the drawer. A glint of amber caught my eye, shimmering like a glassy pond at sunset. I slid the drawer open all the way. I'll be damned—Black Label. I'd forgotten all about it.

I raised the bottle in a silent salute to Merle, then tossed back a single slug. It was a warm bolt of courage going down.

3

I didn't get to Phoebe and Johnnie's until minutes before the clock struck twelve. First, I swung by the Mint to see if Barney was working. He wasn't. They told me he was scheduled for the next day, though, so I figured I'd come back then. New Year's Eve revelry was beginning to reach a fever pitch. I celebrated with a cheeseburger and fries at the Hot 'N Hunky outlet next door, and listened as the mostly male crowd slurred the words to half a dozen beloved old show tunes.

Then I went to the movies. I like to do that on holidays. This time I checked out *Dracula*, the Coppola version, an extravagant failure with its overwrought visuals and gory excess. It was all pretty silly, but Gary Oldman was awfully suave in his topcoat and shades–and I'd watch Winona Ryder in anything.

At the stroke of midnight, I was gnawing on Phoebe's neck and mugging, "I am *Draaa*-coo-lah!"

"Fury, you've got to work on that Transylvania accent." Johnnie was giving us the hairy eyeball over the rim of her martini glass.

"Killjoy." I sidled over to spread around the affection, then pivoted to check out the scene below.

The three of us were perched high on a deck overlooking San Francisco and the world. The Twin Peaks vantage point faced north by northeast; Market Street was a diagonal line heading straight to the bay, cars moving in both directions like tiny illuminated ants. I could see downtown skyscrapers, industrial flatlands, the shadowy hills of the East Bay, and the warm electric glow of a thousand and one apartments. Shivering, I listened to the distant peel of laughter, horns, and music that marked the cusp of another year.

Behind us, through sliding glass doors, Phoebe and Johnnie's townhouse was a relic from another decade. Low rectangular rooms, modular furniture, pole lamps with silver cones poking up like clusters of metallic flowers. Johnnie Blue had begun dressing to match the place, in sleeveless sheaths and pegged slacks with zippers down the side. Very Mary Tyler Moore. Only Johnnie's African-American.

Phoebe was her same old Anglo self—cropped dark hair, peaches 'n' cream complexion, black-checked chef's pants and a T-shirt that read, "Lesbian Avengers: We Recruit." They made quite a pair, the rising star and the taxi driver. I was glad they were my pals, but when I gazed down at the sea of twinkling lights, I felt a dull pain take hold at the base of my throat.

"Have you heard from Tammie Rae?" Phoebe asked. She must have been reading my mind. Rae was a recent heartthrob of mine who now lived in Tennessee.

"Nah."

"Anyone new on the scene?"

"Nope. I'm not really interested."

Johnnie and Phoebe traded a look. I socked 'em each in the shoulder. "Hey! Just because *you* guys are the Blissful Couple doesn't mean we all have to sell out—"

"Sell out?!" Johnnie dropped her jaw in mock outrage.

"Yeah." I grinned wickedly. "Home ownership, joint bank account, family vacations—you're turning out just like the Huxtables!"

The two of them gave me hell for a while, then Johnnie offered to freshen our drinks. Phoebe said sure. I declined, but requested a few more olives. I settled on a squarish turquoise settee that wheezed air when I bounced on the cushions.

While Johnnie banged around in the kitchen, Phoebe filled me in on her progress as an aviatrix. Phoebe was learning to fly at the San Carlos airport. She'd be ready to solo in a few weeks. I couldn't believe it. Just yesterday, it seemed, she'd begun sporting that stupid khaki cap with the little protective ear flaps. Now she was a pilot. It killed me.

"What are you thinking, Nellie?" Phoebe's eyes were steady on mine.

"Nothing."

"Yeah, right."

We were silent. I smiled at my friend. She laughed and said, "So what's up with Pinky?"

Pinky Fury, my teenage daughter, was about to graduate from high school in London. Last time I saw her, she'd forsaken her spiked, Day-Glo pink hairdo in favor of a soft brunette bob. She'd worn no more than three earrings at a time. Her poetry was appearing in more and more publications. I was dying to have her back in town.

Now, Pinky was trying to decide whether to stay in England or head home to the States. In either case, she was planning to postpone college for a little while. I was lobbying hard for good old Frisco by the Bay. Other forces were urging her to stay put. "No word yet," I said, shrugging.

Phoebe said, "I'll send her a letter. I can be very persuasive."

"That's no lie." I hugged her. "Thanks."

Johnnie came back with two martinis and a miniature tray of cocktail olives for me. I chewed one. It was time to hit the road, but Johnnie was asking about my new case. I reiterated what I'd told Phoebe.

"Kent Kishida—" Johnnie paused. "He was Japanese?"

"Yeah, well, his father was Japanese-American and his mother's Chicana. I think. That's what the guy I'm working for said."

"Hmmm." Phoebe was looking at her lover. "You think it was a hate crime?"

Johnnie lifted her shoulders and responded, "You bet. Of one sort or another."

Phoebe shifted her gaze to me.

I nodded.

"I'm trying to remember," Johnnie went on, "Kishida was in the Army, right? And he was gay?"

"Shit, just like that man in Japan!" Phoebe blurted.

I corrected her. "Actually, that guy, Schindler—he was in the Navy. And Kent Kishida wasn't in the Army, either. He was a civilian employee of the military, working maintenance. Which doesn't mean some Army guys couldn't have had it in for him."

The conversation was depressing me. It was a new year, with a new administration, but the winds of change were dormant, as still as a predator moments before the kill. On top of that, my shin was throbbing, the Naugahyde settee kept squeaking and wheezing, and Johnnie had had the audacity to drop an instrumental version of "Auld Lang Syne" into the CD player.

I stood up and tossed a curl out of my eyes. Phoebe

gripped me extra hard as we said goodbye. I thanked them both and beat a hasty retreat.

I was driving a Datsun B210 these days, a mud-colored monster that was a hand-me-down from my journalist friend Lydia Luchetti. I'd helped her out of a jam some time ago—heck, I'd saved her life—and she had rewarded me with this dented-up hatchback. My former vehicle had bit the dust in the line of duty, so I was glad to take the bucket of bolts off her hands.

I decided to swing through the Castro on my way home to Ramona Avenue. I motored the Datsun through a maze of curving streets. Luchetti's old car had a pretty decent tape deck. I cranked the volume and sailed down the bobsled-like run of upper Market, crooning along as a band from Minneapolis belted something about a runaway train. Seattle wasn't the only town with a handle on teen spirit. By the time I veered onto 18th Street, I was feeling revved up, perfectly awake.

The sidewalks were peppered with New Year's Eve stragglers, the bars still humming with activity. I followed Diamond up a steep rise until I hit 20th Street. It was quieter up here, away from the commercial heart of the Castro. I clicked off the music and rolled down the window for a better view.

Bartholomew Lane's building was a broad Victorian that wrapped around the corner, rising at its highest to four stories. Bay windows jutted from the front apartments; an exterior staircase with decorative metal railings snaked up the side. The nearest streetlamp cast a semicircle of light on the structure, showcasing a sophisticated paint job of pale gray, white, and black. I gazed at the darkened windows of the ground floor, corner unit. Laney had said that was his.

Kent Kishida's body had been found just a few blocks

away, where Cumberland Street abutted Noe. According to Laney, there had been no signs of struggle at Kishida's apartment. The police figured he'd been out for a walk—or on his way someplace—when he was ambushed. Forensics indicated he'd been killed at the same spot his body was found.

Still, I wanted to check out the distance from the apartment building to the murder site. I drove a few blocks, coming to rest again where cement steps zigzagged up a slope through an urban patch of garden. It was even quieter over here. No one else was out cruising, much less sitting on a front stoop, pondering resolutions. The tail end of Cumberland Street sat above. Kishida was discovered near the top of the stairs. Altogether, it would have been about a five-minute walk from here to his apartment.

I cut the engine and hopped out at curbside. From this angle, in the dead of night, the little swatch of greenery looked sinister, its silhouette of aloe plants and ivy as forbidding as a dip in a shark tank.

I glanced around nervously. From over the crest of Noe Street, I heard the staccato pop of firecrackers and a follow-up round of laughter. Then silence. I turned and took the steps two at a time. There was nothing to see at the spot Kishida was killed besides trampled dirt, shrubs, and the looming hulk of the Sutro radio tower. There were plenty of homes within shouting distance, however. Funny—Laney told me no one had reported hearing a thing the night of Kishida's death.

I spent a moment absorbing the stillness. When another burst of fireworks broke the fragile calm, I sprinted to the Datsun and pointed it homeward. I kept the windows shut tight all the way.

4

I stopped at my office the next morning before going to see Barney. I wanted to read the news clips that Bartholomew Lane had left with me. Plus, I had ongoing cases that needed maintenance: employee background checks for a sportswear manufacturer; surveillance in a personal-injury suit; and quality control for a chain of upscale espresso outlets.

My work was nearly complete in the first two jobs, but the coffee gig would last through March. It was the easiest—and most trifling—work I'd ever had as a rent-a-cop. Basically, I was supposed to frequent Cuppa? franchises throughout the Bay Area, drink their coffee, eat their pastries, and write reports about the products and services.

So far, the only drawback was the insufferably cheery greeting of "Cuppa?" that employees were required to emote.

Well, that and the fact that my Cuppa? beat extended clear from Petaluma to Santa Cruz. I'd have to put some miles on the Datsun, but at least I'd get plenty of caffeine and carbohydrates for my efforts.

Cuppa? execs had warned me that outlets would be closed on January 1. What a hardship. I tried my luck instead at a dive on Taylor Street called the Muffin Coffee Shop. The donut and coffee were nowhere near Cuppa? standards, but the joint had one big advantage—a downright surly counterman. I gave him a grin and a 100 percent tip, and rode the elevator contentedly to the fifth floor.

No sign of Merle, or anyone else for that matter. My office smelled faintly of ammonia and lemon. I cracked a window and got right to business. Two hours later, I'd typed a few background checks and organized a folder of surveillance photos for my client, the ambulance chaser. I carefully filed everything in my spanking new cabinet. Just as I was turning my attention to Kent Kishida, the telephone rang.

"Fury Investigations."

"Hey, you're working—"

"Lydia. What's up?"

"I need to talk to you, Nell."

"Shoot."

"I mean, in person. How about dinner?"

I swiveled my desk chair and pondered the proposition. Through the freshly cleaned windows, the sky was a palette of unbroken gray. Down along Market Street, a row of dingy storefronts advertised fast food, Levi's, precision haircuts. I could see a posse of pigeons on the nearest rooftop, maniacally pecking at the gravel.

Lydia Luchetti was a full-time newshound for the *San Francisco Chronicle*. She also contributed features to more progressive rags, like the feminist monthly *Re-View*. With Luchetti, it was never a mere social call.

"Okay, dinner," I said. "But give me a hint. What are you looking for?"

She chuckled. "Nell, you're so suspicious."

"No I'm not. I'm just crabby."

More chortling. "Okay, look, you know Peko Muncie, right?"

"Uh-huh." Muncie's a private eye.

"And you know about SLAPP suits?"

"Ummm . . ." I tapped the space bar a few times. The Royal sounded like a nail gun shooting blanks. "Refresh me."

"Strategic Lawsuit Against Public Participation—SLAPP. It's a kind of lawsuit most often filed by a powerful organization against an underdog, usually to stop public dissent. Like when that sanitation company in the East Bay sued a group of neighbors who were speaking out against a garbage burning plant—"

"Yeah, I remember."

"Good. So you know they're mostly frivolous lawsuits. The big guns don't really expect to win, they just want to drain the little guys of money and resources. Intimidate community activists until they're afraid to exercise their First Amendment rights . . ."

I smiled. Luchetti was on a soapbox. It was all coming back to me, though. I recalled a case involving the National Organization for Women. They'd been sued by the State of Missouri when NOW endorsed a boycott of states that hadn't ratified the Equal Rights Amendment. Missouri's suit had been thrown out of court, but not before sapping a lot of NOW's energy.

Luchetti was spouting other examples. Whew—the woman was a font of information. I butted in. "All right, Lydia, I got it. SLAPPs, Peko Muncie. What's the connection?"

"That's what I need you for, Nell. I want to pick your brain. There's a new SLAPP brewing in the City—" Luchetti paused, then lowered her voice "—but let's save it for later, okay? Dinner's on me."

We picked a time and place, and traded goodbyes.

I turned away from the window and flipped open a file folder. Finally, a chance to read the Kent Kishida articles.

The clippings contained little information I hadn't already learned from Bartholomew Lane. Except for one thing. According to an intrepid reporter for the *SF Weekly,* Kishida had been frequenting town hall meetings about toxic-waste problems at the Presidio. He'd also become active in a newly formed coalition of Pacific Heights and Marina residents concerned about what was happening at the old military base. The Presidio, a prime piece of real estate at the northernmost tip of San Francisco, was in the process of changing hands from the military to the National Park Service. Apparently, Kishida's coalition was serving as a watchdog group during the transition period.

The reporter found it odd that Kishida, a Presidio employee, had been involved with outside agitators. He also expressed frustration at the S.F.P.D. Neither the cops nor other local newspapers seemed to think Kishida's murder had anything to do with his nascent community involvement.

Hmm. Laney thought it did. That's why he hired me.

I jotted a few notes, including the name of the homicide inspector in charge of the Kishida case—Elvia Penayo. Then I contemplated strategy. Trips to the cop house, the Presidio, and Bartholomew Lane's apartment building were certainly in order. I'd have to talk to Kishida's neighborhood group. And maybe to Carmelinda Kishida. From there, I'd simply follow the yellow brick road.

When I stepped outside, another horde of pigeons dominated the sidewalk, hunting and pecking like vultures at the scene of a slaughter. The sky remained the color of dirty socks. I made a pit stop at the corner *taqueria,* rescued the B210, and zigzagged out of the Tenderloin, eating and driving at the same time.

5

I walked into the Mint at 1:15, futilely wiping a guacamole stain from the front of my overcoat. Barney announced "Happy New Year!" and slapped a root beer onto the pitted bartop. I grinned and bent low for a sip, licking a foam moustache as I rose to survey the scene.

The bar was almost empty. Everyone must have burned out the night before. A sour, beery waft lingered in the air and a string of holiday lights above the bar blinked erratically like embers dying at a campfire. The jukebox, quiet and solemn as a funeral dirge, droned Traffic's "The Low Spark of High-Heeled Boys."

Barney was a strapping fellow with coal-black skin and a chain-link tattoo that snaked from ear to elbow. Today he wore a fuschia tank top with Tina Turner silkscreened on the front. I cradled my root beer in two hands and said, "How's it going, Barn?"

The chain links rippled when he shrugged. "Okay. Can't complain. You hear they named a dinosaur after me?"

"What?"

"A dinosaur! You know, for kids. It's purple!"

"Well that suits you," I said, humoring him. I didn't know what the hell he was talking about. "Any other ground-breaking news?"

"Naw. Same old." Barney worked a bar rag over a sticky spot. "Are you here about Laney?"

"No, to see you." I flashed a lopsided smile. "*And* about Laney."

He guffawed. Then he got serious. Shaking his bowling ball head, he said, "Laney's hurtin'. Damn—he got sick so fast."

"How long have you known him?"

"Forever. We were in the Gay Men's Chorus together, back in the old days. And I'd see him around town, you know? But at that dinner party the other night, shit . . ." Barney trailed off.

"That's when you gave him my name?"

He nodded. "That all right? He seemed to need advice. Or *something.*"

"Sure. Barney, did you know Kent Kishida?"

"Naw. Laney talked about him all the time. That's all I knew."

"You mean after the murder?"

"Both—before and after. 'Scuse me, Nellie."

Barney sidled down the bar to quench somebody's thirst. I slurped soda. *Before* the murder?

When he came back I asked, "Before the murder?"

"Yeah. Laney was obsessed with the kid. Didn't he tell you?"

"No, he said they were just friends."

"Well, exactly, that was the problem."

"Mmmm." I twirled a stray hank of hair, tucked it behind my ear. "What's your theory on the murder? Gay-bashing?"

Barney was a placid man who loved his pet boxer, his customers, and a finger of peppermint schnapps at closing time. But when I posed the question, a street fight started to rumble behind his umber eyes. He monotoned, "Kishida was a pretty young thing; a hotshot, from what I hear. Yeah, uh-huh. I think it was a gay-bash. Maybe an anti-Japanese thing. Maybe both."

Barney swiped at another spot on the bar, this one imaginary, bearing down on the rag as if it were sandpaper. I said, "Weird that none of the neighbors heard anything."

"Not true."

I peered at Barney. "What?"

"Talk to a lady named Charley. Last name Canton, I think. Charley Canton."

"Who's she?"

"She's got a black Lab, gorgeous animal. We both walk our dogs in Dolores Park. You start talking with the regulars after a while, you know?" Barney planted his elbows on the bartop. I could still see the fight in his eyes. "None of this made the papers, but Charley *did* hear something that night. She lives at the end of Cumberland, above the staircase. She heard raised voices–I'm not sure what all. She told the cops. I guess they wanted to keep it quiet."

"Hunnh." I licked the last trace of foam from my mug. "Does Laney know about her?"

"I don't know, Nell. Maybe."

"Okay Barn. Charley Canton."

I offered to pay for my root beer, but Barney wouldn't have it. I hung around for a while and tried to cheer him up, but it took a trio of pals in sequins and fake lashes to get his mind off race hatred and homophobia. I left. Outside, an early twilight settled on the city like urban grime on an April snow.

* * *

I drove to Ramona Avenue and ditched the Datsun curbside. No parking enforcement today—yee haw. Being a holiday, there was also no mail. Damn.

Tammie Rae Tinkers had been gone for more than a year and I still approached the mailbox with equal parts desire and trepidation. Every day was a love lottery. I don't know what I wanted more—a letter of eternal devotion or a final kiss-off. As it stood, we had a pleasant, ongoing bond, with zero expectations.

Rae was working as an engineer in Nashville. She didn't know if she'd ever move back to San Francisco; I certainly had no plans for Music City. It was a stalemate. I could practically hear the lonely twang of a country ballad when I thought about it too long.

I ignored the barren mailbox and climbed to my dinky attic apartment. Flannery and Carson were two brilliant sunbursts in the otherwise dreary space. I sprinkled some fish chow and watched them hustle to the surface like frenzied shoppers on a tear. Then I circled the room, flicking on lights. Over by the kitchenette, I lifted the telephone, punched a familiar number, and asked for Homicide Inspector Elvia Penayo.

She wasn't at work, so I left a message for her to call me. I tried to reach Tad, too—again, no luck. Tad Greenblatt was an old p.i. buddy and a steady pipeline of information. I thought he might know something about Kishida's murder and the S.F.P.D.'s response. But it would have to wait.

I hefted the phone book and flipped to the Cs. There were a bunch of Cantons, including a C. Canton on Cumberland Street. Touché. I hit seven digits and listened to the melodious rings.

A woman's voice barked, "Hello?"

Hmm. A little testy. "Is Charley Canton there, please?" I asked evenly.

She managed to spit out "Yeah" before dropping the receiver with an ear-splitting clatter. I jerked the phone away from my head. Uh-oh.

Somebody else came on the line, blew a big sigh, and whispered, "Amanda, you can't call here—"

"Hang on. I'm not Amanda—"

"What?!" she blustered.

Geez—now she was pissy, too. I said, "Are you Charley Canton?"

"Y-yes. Who's this?"

"I'm Nell Fury. A friend of mine, Barney—big guy with a little boxer dog—he gave me your name."

"Oh. Shoot. I'm sorry, Dawn said . . . oh, never mind." She sighed and seemed to recover her cool. "Yeah, I know Barney. What do *you* want?"

"Ms. Canton, I'm a private investigator. Barney told me you overheard something the night Kent Kishida died. I'd like to ask you a few questions about it."

Charley heaved another deep sigh. Wow. Her lungs sure got a steady workout. Finally she said, "Look, I already talked to the police."

"I understand. But, as you may know, the case is still open. I'm just checking out some loose ends. For a friend of Kent's," I added, trying to make it sound legit.

Charley Canton utilized more than her fair share of oxygen before agreeing to meet with me. She said tomorrow afternoon, at her place, would be best. She gave me her address and hung up abruptly.

I frowned at the telephone mouthpiece, placed it gently in its cradle, then crashed on the couch to read a few chapters of Carla Tomaso's *The House of Real Love*. It was sad and hilarious—I wished I had a Connie of my own to obsess over. Up close, I mean. When it was time to go to dinner, I pulled a baggy white sweater over my rolled-up jeans, slung on my coat, and headed out into the night.

6

Lydia Luchetti was already seated at the Thai restaurant when I arrived seven minutes ahead of schedule. I smiled at the host, skirted a white bamboo railing, and approached her table. She was nibbling grilled chicken on a stick, but when she saw me, she lept up and smothered me in a squeeze.

This was new behavior for Luchetti—she used to be brisk and reserved. Since recovering from a near-fatal shooting, she'd become much more demonstrative, especially with me, her savior. I waited for her display of affection to subside, then slid into the chair across from her.

"Hiya, Nell. Sorry I didn't wait. I was so hungry, I ordered an appetizer." Lydia pushed the plate across the table. "Here, have some. It's satay, it's fantastic."

A bullet to the brain hadn't dampened her enthusiasm,

that's for sure. Luchetti was as energetic as ever. I thanked her and snagged a stick. Yup, it was tasty all right. When the waiter came by, we ordered dinner and a carafe of red wine. When the wine arrived, I poured out two glasses, clinked mine against Lydia's, and said, "Okay Luchetti. I'm all ears."

"Great." She let her eyes dart around the room. Only three other tables were occupied; she seemed satisfied the place was spy-free. Still, she proceeded in a hush, leaning close to punctuate each sentence with a florid hand gesture like a traffic cop caught in a rush-hour snarl.

"Okay, you know Peko Muncie's a private eye. Works for that slime-dog outfit, uh, what's it called—"

"E-Z—"

"E-Z Investigative Services. Right. So, I'm doing a story on a new organization called NTWA. Neighborhood Toxic Waste Alert. It's an umbrella group trying to organize communities throughout the city. You heard of it, Nell?"

"No." I swallowed a hunk of satay and chased it with wine.

"Hmmpph," Lydia chided, half in jest. "You didn't read your *Chron* last Sunday."

"Oops. Guess I was too busy catching up on *I ♡ Amy Carter.*"

"Well, what you missed was my first story about NTWA— its formation, goals, key players, that kind of thing. Pulitzer Prize material, hear what I'm saying?"

I laughed.

Lydia chuckled too. Her smooth auburn bob swished gently against her cheeks. Her eyes looked wet in the subdued light of the restaurant. Suddenly I wondered if Luchetti was flirting with me. I tugged at my napkin and said hurriedly, "So, you're doing a follow-up story on this toxic waste group?"

She nodded, businesslike again. "Yeah, I'm doing a series. That's the thing. NTWA had a meeting on Tuesday night, this

Tuesday, after my story ran on Sunday. And Peko Muncie was there, undercover. *Trying* to be undercover, that is."

I smiled. E-Z operatives weren't known for their finesse, Muncie included. "Someone made him."

"Uh-huh. This guy, Christopher Mason, who I talked to for the first story, he recognized Muncie in spite of—or maybe *because* of—his L.L. Bean get-up. Too clean, you know? Christopher had seen Muncie on some schlock TV show—'Hard Copy,' I think. So he called to tell me Muncie was at their meeting."

"Any chance Peko Muncie's just another citizen concerned about environmental pollution?" I didn't believe it for a second, but I wanted to check Lydia's response. She howled.

"That's a good one. No. NTWA thinks he's a mole. And they want me to expose him in print."

I shrugged. "Sounds like your kind of thing."

"Yeah." Lydia's eyes glistened. "It is. I might even confront him directly, but I wanted to ask around first, maybe find out some dirt before putting him on the defensive. But there's a problem."

"What?"

"Oh, Nell." Luchetti sighed, smiling at me sideways. Then she reached a hand across the table, almost toppling her wine glass in the rush to invade my personal space. She gripped my wrist and said, "I mentioned it to Meg, just casually, in conversation. And she freaked out! She told me to forget about Muncie and just write my stupid story. Those were her words, my 'stupid story'!"

"Uh-oh," I muttered, removing Luchetti's paw and downing a healthy gulp of water. Margaret Halliway—Meg—was Luchetti's longtime lover. She was also District Attorney for the City and County of San Francisco. Lydia once told me they were careful to keep clear boundaries between their professional and personal lives. But this sounded like one big messy personal-professional clash.

Lydia said, "Damn, sometimes I don't think it's worth it anymore," then treated me to another bittersweet grin.

"Why was Meg so touchy about Peko Muncie?"

"She wouldn't say, but I think I know what's going on. Meg told me a while ago the City was planning to file lawsuits against certain activist groups on all these bogus charges: defamation, conspiracy, interference with business. Even abuse of judicial process, if you can believe that—"

"What kind of organizations?"

"Oh, god, everything from ACT-UP to public-school advocacy groups. And now, apparently, Neighborhood Toxic Waste Alert. It's really fucked-up. I accused Meg of orchestrating SLAPP suits, and *she* got mad at *me*—accused me of being knee-jerk. She really believes the City has a right to target groups that, quote, 'hurt its image.' And to try and get money out of those people, as if that'll be enough to balance the city budget. You know what I think?" Lydia brandished her arm in a rhetorical flourish. "I think Meg's a pawn. I think the cops and the mayor are using her as a legal tool to squelch public dissent. And she's going along! It's textbook SLAPP strategy."

Luchetti paused for air. I glanced at our table, cluttered with empty plates, tin serving dishes, soiled napkins. I still didn't know exactly what Luchetti wanted from me, a common problem these days. I cleared a spot for my elbow and asked, "So you and Meg haven't resolved this?"

"Nope. I'm pissed and she won't talk about it. The thing is, I think Meg, or one of her assistant D.A.'s, hired Muncie to infiltrate NTWA. Makes you wonder who else the City is spying on."

I murmured assent. Lydia's melty eyes were all over me. Again, I wondered if she was courting my affections or about to solicit a favor. With Luchetti, maybe it was one and the same thing.

"Nell," she said, interrupting my train of thought, "do you think you can find out if I'm right? If Peko Muncie was hired by the City and, if so, what for? It'd really help my series—"

"You're saying you want me to check up on your lover? Behind her back?"

She ducked her head. "I know, it sounds bad. But I think I can do a decent job of exposing SLAPP suits for what they are—malicious attempts to abridge the First Amendment! And Margaret . . . I think it's curtains for us, anyway."

For the first time all night, Lydia Luchetti appeared genuinely grieved. Her shoulders shook a little, her lips so tight that creases fanned out around them like the pinched corners of cellophane shrinkwrap. I held her gaze, my own feelings caught somewhere between empathy and caution.

We were quiet as the waiter cleared our dishes, dragged the tablecloth with a little metal scraper, and disappeared with Luchetti's plastic. He reappeared to complete the phantom transaction. When it was over, I told Lydia I'd ask around about Muncie. I had a direct bead on E-Z Investigative Services through an old colleague named Darnelle Comey. Besides, I try to make a habit of agreeing to small favors. This business is a nonstop hustle of back-scratching and hunch-playing; you never know when a little task will net a big fish somewhere down the line.

"Thank you, Nell!" Lydia gushed. We shook on it. Luchetti's imploring eyes kept making me squirm. When she asked if I wanted to go someplace for coffee, I said no thanks.

It was still early when we parted on Valencia Street. I decided to swing by Wild Side West for a nightcap and a bit of diversion. The Cortland Street hole-in-the-wall was stuffed with locals, sports fans, dykes, and drifters, and everybody got along, or put on a good show of it. Even if there are no lesbian bars left in Everybody's Favorite City, at least there are refuges like this where it's easy to blend in with the land-scape.

I killed an hour in the smoky cave wishing Rae would materialize, pool cue in hand, and ask me to rack 'em up. It didn't happen. I called it a night.

7

The little green light on my phone machine was flashing hypnotically when I got home. I decided to postpone my encounter with the Nell Fury Fan Club and head straight for the sheets. Moments later, it seemed, the diffuse light of another winter morning was filtering through my tiny attic window. I blinked. The clock said 8:14.

The shower was warm and welcome. I stood there, lathered with Biolage and rose-scented soap, and twisted the radio dial. The waterproof gadget was a recent gift from my newly attentive brother Harry. For a few days, I'd gotten a kick out of musical bathing. Now I was tiring of the novelty. Besides, all I could find this morning was Whitney Houston belting her undying devotion to Kevin Costner. I practiced hitting the high notes with Whitney, then clicked the damn thing off.

My shin would be okay without a Band-Aid, so I tossed Betty Boop. I toweled off, pulled on my white sweater, and belted up a pair of oversized brown trousers. I found my battered turquoise cowboy boots under the bed, and slipped on my glasses to complete the get-up. Afterwards, I headed to the front room to listen to my messages.

Madeline Zule Fury—a.k.a. Pinky—was first. "Hey mum!" she began, voice crackling across transatlantic wires. It was a brief happy-new-year call, but it made my heart skip a beat all the same. Tad Greenblatt was next, also heralding the holiday. He mentioned, too, that he'd be out of town until Monday and, no, he knew nothing special about Kent Kishida. The next caller was Bartholomew Lane—I'd given him both my home and office numbers. He was just checking in, he said. Finally, there was a beep and some static, but no message. Rae? Ha. It was probably just a wrong number.

I called Laney back, got his machine, and told him I'd know more later in the day.

On a hunch, I called my office and punched in the code to retrieve messages from the answering machine. The first beep led to a shower of praise from the sportswear tycoon who'd hired me for employee background checks. She said she loved my neat, tidy reports. I guffawed, glancing around my efficiency apartment with its post-tornado decorator's touch. If she only knew. The second beep was Merle, just checking up on her new fifth-floor neighbor. "Give a knock!" she enthused. "Toodle-oo!"

The third beep snapped me to attention.

"Ms. Nell Fury? This is Elvia Penayo, S.F.P.D. Homicide. Call me promptly. I won't have private parties interfering with police work." Click.

Whoa. Private party? I hadn't told her my profession. She must have floated my name around the department.

I returned the call. Penayo was indeed at work on Saturday. She came roaring over the phone like a Circuit City salesperson at the height of a pitch.

"Fury?"

"Yes, Inspector, I—"

"Listen, do you have any information for me? 'Cause if you don't, I'm not wasting my time with a dime-store snoop. I know about you, Fury, you got a reputation around here, know what I'm saying? So what is it? Shoot. Make it snappy."

"Inspector Penayo, I—"

"Don't 'Inspector' me. You got something to say or not?"

Hmmph. If she thought Intimidation 101 would work on me, she had a few things to learn about Nell Fury, Dime-Store Snoop. I leaned against the counter, crossed one cowboy boot over the other, and admired the way the turquoise looked against the black-and-white kitchenette tiles. I said: "Kent Kishida."

"Jeee-sus."

"No. Kishida."

"Look here," Penayo fumed, "the Kishida case is dead in the water. Unless you got a confession—signed, sealed, and delivered—you're not gonna get to play bounty hunter on this one!"

I thought fast. What did I really want from her? "I know about Carmelinda Kishida," I ventured. "Her paranoid phone call. And Kent's sudden interest in environmental affairs. Rather odd, wouldn't you say?"

"Ms. Fury," Penayo said soothingly, switching tactics abruptly. Aha. I knew it was an act all along. She went on, "Of course the case *appears* to have its quirks. Don't they all? But, really, Kishida's mother, she's just a little *loca,* you know what I'm saying? And the other stuff—all a dead end. We figure it was just a random mugging. Tragic. Very tragic."

"So there's nothing more to be done?"

"Oh, we're still hoping for a break, but after two

months?" She sucked air. "You know how cold a trail can get."

She was playing me for a sucker, that much I knew. I wondered if the case really was stagnant, or if the department just wanted to keep "private parties" from prying too closely. And if so, why? I said smoothly, "You had some lesbian and gay activists breathing down your neck, didn't you? For failing to aggressively pursue this as a gay-bashing–"

"Hey, we've got all kinds of people breathing down our necks, believe me. I wish Kishida was the only stiff we had to worry about."

Hmm, finally a genuine sentiment. I said: "Truce, okay? I just called as a professional courtesy. Since we're after the same thing–"

"I doubt that." Penayo hung up.

I looked at the receiver. It was becoming a habit of mine. A newsprint smudge the shape of a nuclear mushroom cloud marred the otherwise spotless white plastic. I depressed the button and waited for a new dial tone, then called the number Laney had given me for Carmelinda Kishida. No answer. Just in case, I called Watsonville directory assistance and checked Mrs. Kishida's number. They gave me the same seven numerals. When I dialed again and waited through twenty rings, there was still no answer.

My head was starting to throb with caffeine withdrawal. One more call and I'd head out for a Cuppa?.

It was a bit early to phone on a weekend, but Darnelle Comey was forever indebted to me for career guidance and good sportsmanship. At any rate, that's how I saw it. Evilly, I punched in her number.

Darnelle answered groggily on the second ring. "Hullo?"

"Hey, squirt. It's Nell Fury."

"Nell!"

"I didn't wake you, did I?"

"Unh, uh-uh." I heard another muffled voice in the background. Oops. "No," Darnelle continued, "I'm . . . awake."

"Good." I made a sloppy figure eight with the phone cord. "Want to have supper with me tonight? Tomato sandwiches—extra mayo—at my place? Eight o'clock?"

Darnelle almost squealed. "Yes!!"

I chuckled. Here I was, planning to grill her for info, and Darnelle was as thrilled as a baby dyke on her way to Michigan for the first time. She was okay, though. We'd met a few years ago when she was a junior detective and I was a hardened p.i.—at least in Darnelle's eyes. I'd taught her some tricks of the trade and she had adored me ever since.

"Can I bring anything?" she asked.

"Ummm, Fritos and—" I had a sudden flash. Maybe Darnelle Comey could help in more ways than one. "And a notebook."

"What—"

"Eight o'clock sharp. Be there or—"

"O-*kaaay*. See ya, Nell!"

The Datsun coughed a bit of smoke when I fired her up. I patted the dash, idled a while, and popped Carlene Carter into the tape deck. Long before the recent surge in popularity of women in Nashville, Carter proclaimed she was proud to "put the cunt back in country." I couldn't have said it better myself. I hummed along, rubbing my fingerless gloves together to generate some warmth. Then I released the brake and rolled north towards the Presidio.

I tried to visit a new Cuppa? almost every day. So far, I'd checked out most of the franchise stores in and around my neighborhood, but I'd never been to the outlet in Laurel Heights. And it was right on the way.

The little commercial zone was quiet for a Saturday. I spied the trademark burlap bean bags and trendy Italian coffeemakers on display in the Cuppa? window. Steeling myself for the inevitable good cheer, I strolled into the cozy storefront like any other shopper in search of a pick-me-up.

"Cuppa?" said the lad behind the counter with the candy-apple cheeks and pert red bowtie.

No, I thought meanly, a whole pot. But I simply said "Yeah," knocking off another rigorous obligation in the glamour game of private investigation.

8

Twenty minutes later I was chugging north on Presidio Avenue. The double latte had been better than average, the chocolate-raspberry scone absurdly delicious. I motored through the stone gate at Presidio and Pacific Avenue and checked out the sights as the block of spiffy urban homes gave way to a suddenly lush parkland of rolling hills and trees.

The Presidio—which literally means "walled fort"—was a desolate stretch of sand and mud when Spanish forces staked out the land as a military base in the 1700s. A century later, after Mexico ruled the fort for a while, the U.S. Army wrested control. The new landowners planted trees to function as a wind break and to delineate the military enclave from the rest of the city. Now the sprawling region was a jumble of eucalyptus and other non-native vegetation I couldn't identify. To me it was a scenic hodgepodge accompanied by an equally varied mix of architectural styles.

Adobe, wood, straw, and brick were some of the materials used over the years to construct the military encampment, though the Spanish mission style of crisp white adobe and terra cotta roofs seemed to predominate. Today, the base still headquartered the Sixth U.S. Army and various reserve units, its fifteen hundred acres bustling with military activities of dubious purpose. Bordered by the Pacific Ocean, the "Bay of Bays," and the wealthiest neighborhoods in San Francisco, the Presidio was an invaluable chunk of property that had always struck me as exclusive, mysterious, and a little bit creepy.

Thanks to legislative hijinks in recent years, the land would go to the National Park Service instead of private developers when the Army officially departed in 1995. The area would be reborn not only as a recreation site, but also as a haven to organizations—for-profit and not—concerned with global peace, AIDS research, bicycle commuting, ecological health, interactive dance, you name it. Gorby had already been to town to stake a claim for his allegedly humanitarian Gorbachev Foundation. No matter who set up shop on the land, I figured the looming ghost of the military's presence would never be completely laid to rest.

I followed a maze of winding curves towards the center of the base. I'd driven these roads on a number of occasions, usually on some sightseeing excursion or another. One time— on a citywide jaunt in search of memorable movie sites— Phoebe and I had ventured through the gates to find the house where Sean Connery and Meg Ryan lived in *The Presidio*. Hey—there it was again! I rolled onto the soft shoulder of Funston Avenue to check out the corner Victorian, really no more distinguished than countless other domiciles around town. Heck, the movie had been a dud too. I shrugged, then took the opportunity to peruse my shopworn AAA map.

I hadn't called the maintenance staff ahead of time: I wanted to catch Kent Kishida's former co-workers off guard. But I had called Presidio Information. They told me the maintenance shed was located off Marina Boulevard, along the main drag that fed traffic toward the Golden Gate Bridge. I followed a circuitous route to get there, swinging by the Presidio's main parade ground with its smooth green lawn, tidy wooden barracks, and a towering flagpole that I knew to be the tallest in the Bay Area. Awe-inspiring, I guess, if you liked your phallic imagery and patriotism all wrapped up in one. I kept my eyes on the road.

The maintenance shed was easy to find. The squat utilitarian building was clearly marked with an official-looking sign and fronted by a row of neatly parked vehicles. I rolled into a visitor's parking spot and alighted onto the blue-black blacktop. The rust-red span of the Golden Gate Bridge stretched like a phony backdrop behind the drab shed. I hoisted my all-purpose briefcase from behind the driver's seat and readied myself for a masquerade.

"Do you need something, ma'am?" said a young buck in army fatigues who stepped across the pavement to greet me. His thighs rubbed together when he walked, toes pointed outward to give all those muscles some room to ripple.

I dove straight into a handshake. "I'm Susan North, from down south. L.A.," I added, twinkling like a maniac. Somehow, I found it easier to pull these stunts while wearing glasses. "My associates and I are pursuing an idea for a television docudrama. *The Kent Kishida Story.*"

Muscle Bound's eyes widened. "You're from Hollywood?"

"Well, Century City, actually." Twinkle, twinkle.

"Kishida?!"

"So you knew him?"

"Sure. But—" He bit his surprisingly pink bottom lip. "You want to make a movie about *him?!*"

"We're thinking about it, yes. It has many dramatic possibilities—gay man, Japanese-American, young fellow just finding his social consciousness. He gets cut down in his prime. No suspects. There are many angles to explore—"

"Yeah, right, all that p.c. shit." He snorted.

I smiled through my irritation. "Can you tell me something about Mr. Kishida? Who his friends were? What he did after hours?"

Muscle Bound retreated a step, flicking his hand dismissively. It could have been a salute or an obscenity. "I don't want anything to do with that fag shit. Talk to Clemens, inside." He wheeled around and headed for the side of the shed.

"Clemens?" I called to his massive green back. "Who's that?"

"Stu Clemens. Crew chief." He didn't even turn around when he said it.

Forget lifting the ban on gay people in the armed forces, I thought annoyedly. Why not ban the whole damn military? I took a few deep breaths and imagined how Susan North would feel. Aggressive and unflappable. Okay, Fury, power on. I pulled my coat collar tight against the chilly breeze and hustled over to the aluminum door at the front of the building.

Inside, the shed felt unnaturally hot, the smell of oil and sweat lingering like the stench of grease in a hash house. About a dozen people were scattered throughout the room, some kicking back, some attending to various duties over desks or heavy equipment. From somebody's work station, a radio spat out the noisy play-by-play of a football game. It was hard to hear over the din.

I stopped at a spindly table to the left of the door and asked a camouflage-clad clone for Stu Clemens. She pointed wordlessly towards the nearest corner where a trio of partitions rose up to form a makeshift office.

I headed that way and shrugged off my overcoat, which

got hopelessly tangled with my briefcase. I paused, threw the coat over one arm, grasped the case under the other, and gave the partitioned office a quick once-over. The outermost panel displayed an army recruiting poster and a pinup calendar bordered in stars and stripes. Miss January sported a fatigue-green g-string, an eagle tattoo over one breast, and a bayonet clutched coyly in the crook of her arm.

"Mr. Clemens?" I called out loudly, stepping forward through the vertical opening.

"Huh?"

"Are you Stu Clemens?"

The man had his mouth around a point of pepperoni pizza. He dropped the slice on a paper plate, then shifted in his chair, legs spread wide, heels bouncing compulsively on a swatch of indoor-outdoor carpeting. He couldn't have been older than thirty, a hard-bitten upstart in civvies and a tie. His beady, red-rimmed eyes looked like two petrified disks of pepperoni.

"Yeah, I'm Stuart Clemens. You a new hire?"

Lord, no, I thought. But I just said: "I'm a TV producer, Mr. Clemens. I understand Kent Kishida worked for you?"

"Huh?"

Hmm. His limited vocabulary might pose a problem. I pushed on, repeating my song-and-dance about the proposed docudrama. Clemens warmed up a little, even offered me a chair and a slab of pizza. I accepted the former, opened my briefcase, extracted a notepad, and asked if Kent Kishida had seemed different in the months before he died. More, uh, socially aware, I said vaguely.

"Kishida? Nah. Unless by 'socially aware' you mean aware of other guys socially." Clemens slapped himself on the thigh.

I smiled a Susan North smile. "So he never talked about . . . environmental concerns? Toxic waste problems at the Presidio, for instance?"

"Ohhh. What's to say? We're all concerned." Miraculously, crude Stuart Clemens transformed into an Army spokesperson right before my eyes. "Toxic waste cleanup has been our number-one priority since the base closure was announced. It's a big problem, sure, but we're on top of it."

I refrained from genuflecting. "What's the problem, specifically?"

Clemens launched into a well-rehearsed monologue about asbestos, underground storage tanks, oil, pesticides, solvents, medical waste, and other poisons permeating the Presidio buildings and grounds. I felt like taking a shower, just hearing him talk. He said the Army had a cleanup budget adequate for the task at hand, and a timeline that satisfied Park Service officials. He pointed to a map pinned above his desk that highlighted primary areas of concern.

He started to mention community disgruntlement and pressure from environmental groups, but stopped himself mid-monologue. Either he got suspicious or figured he was boring me. Or both.

"And you say Kishida wasn't particularly interested in the topic?" I prodded.

Clemens shrugged. "Nope."

"How about his relationships with co-workers? Did they know he was gay?"

"You ever meet the guy?"

I shook my head.

"If you had, you wouldn't have asked." Clemens leaned forward conspiratorially and whispered, "A flaming queen, that guy. I'm not surprised he got offed."

"Oh?"

"Sure, people hate that crap."

"People around here, you mean?" From over the office partition, I heard a whoop of excitement to match the tinny hysteria coming over the radio. Chalk one up for the home team.

"No," Clemens said briskly. "Of course not. Kent was . . . one of the guys. But if Clinton lets in *all* the homosexuals, then there'll be trouble."

I grunted noncommittally. Clemens squirmed, and regained his PR composure. He asked about the docudrama and I lied smoothly for a while, almost convincing myself that Kent Kishida could top Amy Fisher in the TV ratings game. Finally, when we were both fed up with each other, I stood up to leave.

"Thank you, Mr. Clemens. Listen, maybe you know who Kishida hung out with here. I'm hoping to talk to more people, you know, to flesh out his background. Any ideas?"

Clemens' red eyes turned skyward for a moment. "A lady in DEH—that's Department of Engineering and Housing. They oversee the whole maintenance staff, civilian and military. Her name's Rory Rafferty. And another guy on the grounds crew, Trip Hamm." He leaned over to peruse a wall chart. "He's not working today, though. Off 'til Monday."

"Ham?"

"H–A–M–M."

I gave him a Susan North business card with a local contact number—it was my second office phone, unlisted. Then I asked for directions to DEH. I snapped my briefcase shut and left Clemens to his now-cold lunch. I made for the exit and its promise of fresh air, a serenade of echoes and distorted radio noises dogging my steps.

I didn't turn around to check, but I could swear Miss January had her bayonet poised, aiming right for my backside.

9

I found a place to park the Datsun on Cumberland Street, just a few driveways down from the cul-de-sac. The car lurched backwards, hiccupping raucously when I killed the engine. Uh-oh. I set the brake extra tight and checked the time. 2:05 p.m.

My old Elvis watch, which had died a few months ago, was no doubt experiencing a spiritual resurrection somewhere on the grounds of Graceland. Meanwhile, I relied on a Woolworth's special with faux-antique numerals and a tendency to run eight minutes fast. Good. I was right on time for my two o'clock rendezvous with Charley Canton.

Rory Rafferty had not been in when I stopped at the Presidio's Department of Engineering and Housing. I'd left her a message and a Susan North calling card. I'd also looked up Trip Hamm in the city phone directory. No luck. But I had managed to corral a grounds crew busy beautifying a rusty cannon and a pyramid of cannonballs—a futile job, if you asked me. Several of the men said they knew Hamm, and were quick to cough up his phone number when I alluded to lights-camera-action. I figured I'd call him later from the office.

Then I'd sped across town in the little brown slug.

Charley Canton's house was a sleek, contemporary structure in dark stained wood. It was set back from the street, shielded by a riot of trees and dense brush. When I rang the bell, I heard a deep growl kick in from behind the lacquered front door. Must be the famous black Labrador. Moments later, solid footfalls drowned out the dog. The door swung inward. I was looking at a middle-aged knockout who could pass for Isabella Rossellini's big sister. I gulped.

"Nell Fury?" the woman said.

"Rrrf, rrrf!" mimicked the black Lab.

"Shhh," she murmured, her lips forming a cupid's bow as she bent low to soothe the beast. Isabella's Sister glanced up and dazzled me with a smile. Her front teeth were adorably crooked. "Come on in," she said.

I found my vocal cords. "You're Charley?"

"Mmm-hmm. Have a seat in the kitchen while I put him out back."

I followed her part-way down the corridor to the right and settled at a butcher-block counter in the middle of a designer showroom. Copper pans hung from the ceiling; the latest kitchen finery lined a counter inlaid with rustic brick-red tiles. High, arched windows looked to the west, framing a tourist bureau's dream view of steep hills, crisply painted Victorians, forest green foliage, and—today—overcast skies. From here you could see the top ridge of the mini-park where I'd spooked myself on New Year's Eve.

Charley Canton sidled up behind me and whispered, "Like the view?"

I jumped, and felt a tingly heat radiate from my mid-section. What was going on? Canton had been flustered, even irritated, on the telephone, and now she oozed more charm than a figure skater trying to woo the judges. What the heck—maybe she liked women in glasses. I removed my coat, gave her a bemused smile, and said, "The indoor view is nicer."

Charley almost purred with satisfaction as she prepared a complicated brew in one of her shiny electric appliances. I studied her unimpeachable profile and waited while she measured, leveled, steamed, and poured. Finally she set two cappuccinos on the counter and took a seat across from me. I noticed her knuckles were a bit rough, her palms callused.

"What can I do for you, Nell?" she asked, eyes steady over the white enamel cup.

I blushed. That was a good question. Already, this wasn't going the way I'd intended. Maybe we should just dispatch with things here on the butcher-block table, like Lana Turner and John Garfield in *The Postman Always Rings Twice*, then talk murder and mayhem. I blew into my cup. Too hard, apparently, because half the coffee lapped over the rim and slopped onto the counter.

"I'm sorry!" I blurted, scanning frantically for a napkin.

"Hey, don't worry. I've got it." Charley whipped a colorful, hand-dyed cloth from beneath the counter and erased the spill. Then she angled her neck and asked, "Want another?"

"No-o-o." I bolted the remaining coffee in one gulp and felt the hot liquid sear my tongue. Damn. "No, thanks," I winced, biting back the pain. "Listen, I came here to find out what you heard that night, the night Kent Kishida was killed."

"Mmmm." Charley's half-smile was delicate and sad, but confident, too, as if she knew full well the effect she was having on me. "It was unusually warm that night, even for October . . . " she began.

The whole account took less than ten minutes.

In a nutshell: Charley told me she overheard several male voices quarreling that night on the staircase connecting Cumberland to Noe Street. She wandered into the kitchen and peered out the window, but couldn't see anything out of the ordinary. She just figured some neighbors—or passersby—were arguing.

Then Charley heard a sharper noise, like a crack, followed by a scream. She definitely discerned the name Kishida; an angry voice barked it as an epithet. Then a retort that sounded like "mace" or "maze."

None of it registered as important at the time, but when Charley saw the news report the next day, she called the cops. They interviewed her at length—even put her under hypnosis to try and sharpen her memory. The most helpful thing she recalled was that, after the ruckus, two distinct sets of footsteps tripped down the steps and faded from earshot.

"Hunh." I fiddled with the sleeves of my sweater. "Anyone else in the neighborhood hear anything?"

"Apparently not. If so, they didn't speak up."

"Do you know why your story stayed out of the newspapers?"

Charley moistened her upper lip. "I believe the police wanted to keep it secret, you know, to help their investigation. Not that it seemed to."

I arched an eyebrow.

Charley laughed softly, a patter of raindrops on the roof of a tent. "Are you skeptical, too, Nell?"

I didn't care to show my cards. Not then. I said, "What do you mean?"

She walked to the window, treating me to another glimpse of her astonishing profile. I felt a second heat wave ripple down my extremities. I was perspiring in places I didn't know it was possible.

"I think the cops botched it," Charley explained. "From what I overheard, I'd say the man was killed by someone he knew—for some specific reason. But the police don't seem to care. They're acting like it was just a random crime."

"Who did you talk to? I mean, which cops?"

"Umm, a couple of patrol officers. I can't remember their names. And the homicide inspector, I swear, she was something—"

"Elvia Penayo?"

Charley wheeled away from the window and grinned. "You've done your homework."

I feigned nonchalance. "What do you mean, 'she was something'?"

"She's intense, hard-working. But slippery. I never knew what she was thinking." Charley's crooked teeth glinted. "Just like you."

I leaned back on the kitchen stool and crossed a booted foot over one knee. This conversation was helpful in one regard: if Charley Canton was right, then there *was* something fishy about Kishida's murder. My efforts—and Laney's concern—were not all for naught. As for this tortured tête-à-tête, we could have been actors in a cheesy soap opera, the kind in which the producer includes a Sapphic subplot to demonstrate his/her chicness. At the moment, I felt anything but chic, sweating in a stranger's kitchen with a scalded tongue and a battery of questions muddling my overloaded brain.

I was starting to calculate how long it'd been since I'd had sex when Charley asked, "Are you single, Nell?"

I gripped the toe of my boot and grinned. "As a matter of principle."

"Good. So you're . . . available."

"Theoretically." I figured it out—five months. Rae had come to visit last summer.

"What does it take to turn theory into practice?" Charley's arms were crossed below her breasts, her soft brown jacket cut low enough to show an inch of lace at the V-neck. The hollow of her throat looked pale and mysterious, like a strange outcropping of rock caught in a black-and-white photograph.

Suddenly, she wasn't Isabella's sister anymore but Anne Bancroft lounging suggestively in leopardskin, a lit cigarette dangling gallantly from one hand.

"Are you trying to seduce me, Mrs. Robinson?" I queried, ever the wordsmith.

Charley laughed.

All right. Things were going to work out just fine.

I rattled down Church Street marvelling at the rest of Charley Canton's come-on. It was more than I'd bargained for, but hey, I was game. Turns out Charley liked to work in tandem with Dawn, her partner, the short-tempered lass who'd answered the phone when I first called. Charley assured me Dawn was normally quite pleasant; they'd just been wrangling over a recent breakup with Amanda, a woman who had tried to steal Charley from Dawn and screw up a lovely three-way.

"You tiger," I'd growled.

I got confused thinking about the sordid details, but this much I knew: with the sexual liberation movement in constant jeopardy, what was wrong with a nice old-fashioned menage? Heck, it almost felt like a political obligation.

Charley had a thing about anticipation, too. She wanted to wait until Monday. Could she and Dawn take me to lunch and then—? Sure, I'd said. The whole affair took on an added gloss when she suggested Elka, *the* trendy dining spot of the moment. Elka, tailored jackets, fancy digs on Cumberland Street—these gals had liquid gold flowing through their veins. Still, they were a more appealing prospect than Lydia Luchetti. I loved Lydia, but she was making me nervous. And

Princess, an occasional object of my affection in the recent past, had had a commitment ceremony and moved to Marin.

Suddenly ravenous, I popped the glove compartment and found a pack of Licorice Whips in my emergency stash. I chewed, pumping the brakes as I neared the corner of Church and Market. A mess of construction work was tangling up the intersection. I'd heard they were planting palm trees along a four-block stretch of Upper Market. South Beach meets Christopher Street. Go figure. I cranked the wheel, swerved blindly around two Muni buses, and jammed down Market Street all the way to the Tenderloin.

Normally, parking would be a problem at my new office, but vandals had been wreaking havoc on the city's meters, slicing the tops off cleanly with the finesse of a sushi chef. I found a decapitated pole and hopped out of the car. Above me, a sign for the so-called Art Theatre glittered like a carnival marquee, its logo advising, "If you want to do it right, do it yourself. Buy a vibrator. Over 1,000 in stock today." Yup, that's always an option, I thought happily.

Riding the elevator to the fifth floor, I made a mental checklist of the calls I wanted to knock off before my dinner with Darnelle. Laney, Trip Hamm, one more try to Carmelinda Kishida. Maybe I'd see how Phoebe was doing. The rickety cage came to a halt. I slid back the hinged metal gate and headed for the office, fishing my shiny new Schlage key from the depths of my coat pocket.

Unfortunately for me, I ignored one of the principle lessons of private-eye boot camp: always be aware of your surroundings. As I blithely inserted the key into the lock, I felt a presence hovering to my left. I turned, vaguely cognizant of someone tall with a mass of dark hair. Ah, it must be Merle.

Whop!! A blow caught me at the side of the neck. I staggered backwards. S/he was tall, that's for sure, but the dark crown was actually a woolly black ski mask, its cutouts revealing nothing but grim gray lips and horrifically hollow eye sockets. I groped frantically for my briefcase, hoping to use it as a weapon. But a second wallop came quickly, another fist to the head that sent me reeling to the carpet like a woozy drunk, counting stars and wondering idly if Riddick Bowe would have fared any better in my shoes.

10

A naked light bulb was the first thing I saw when I came to. It swayed overhead, a fuzzy orange sun quivering on a chain. Behind it, flecks of yellowed paint peeled in curlicues from a blotchy ceiling. The view wasn't worth the effort. I closed my eyes.

When I opened them a second time, a halo of ebony curls blocked out the ersatz sun. I jerked violently.

"Hey-y-y," a soothing soprano crooned. I felt a tentative palm guide my shoulder back to the floor. I fluttered my eyelashes. The voice said, "Let's see how bad they fucked you up."

I blinked again. I recognized familiar scarlet lips, a matching red bow, generous breasts bound tight in an orange silk bodice. Ahhh. It was Barbie—er, Merle. We seemed to be in the fifth floor hallway of 25 Taylor Street. I took a few exploratory breaths, then reached a hand up to finger my head. Amazingly, my glasses were intact, but a spot behind my left ear felt spongy and matted with blood.

"Ooooo-oo-o-o!" said Merle.

I practiced smiling. "What kind of talent did you say you represent?"

"Really, Nell, we can gossip about business later—ah!" She gasped and raised a hand to her parted mouth. "You don't think one of *my* people did this?"

"No. Just curious." I sat up on one elbow, then collapsed instantly, fighting back a wave of nausea. I squeaked, "Could you get me some water, please?"

Merle bustled down the corridor and returned with two Dixie cups of H_2O. By then, I had arranged myself into a seated position, back flush against the walls, knees to my chest. In some far corner of my brain, I registered the fact that my office door was ajar and the contents of my wallet strewn helter-skelter across the carpet like losing stubs scattered forlornly at the racetrack. My head was a throbbing melon. I pressed the sleeve of my sweater against the sore spot, afraid gray matter might be leeching out.

"Here you go, honey."

I drank.

"Now let me see." Merle peeled away my hand and drew close to examine the wound. "Tsk," she said, fanning back my hair and probing the area with her fingertips. "Doesn't look too bad, but you never know. Could be a concussion."

I rolled my head around on my neck, mentally running through vital stats: my name, k.d. lang's birthday, my favorite David Bowie song, the best place in town for an Irish coffee. Things were moving back into focus. "I think I'll be okay," I said. "But can you help me get cleaned up?"

"Darn tootin'."

Merle assisted me to the bathroom. We pinned my hair out of the way and cleaned the contusion. I also rinsed my face and tried in vain to wash the blood out of my sweater. On the trek back down the hall, it occurred to me to check my watch. Heavens. 11:10 p.m.

"Shit."

"Shit!" agreed Merle, waving wildly in the direction of my office.

"Where'd that tree come from?!" I shrieked, momentarily flummoxed by the gaudy, tropical-looking growth that towered in the corner next to the filing cabinet.

"Not that—I got that for you. Look!"

I stumbled into the room in a daze. My wallet wasn't the only thing plundered. My brand new office was in shambles, drawers emptied, papers dispersed, desk lamp lying on its side, cowering in defeat. Even my Chicago Cubs wall calendar was ripped clean through and dumped in little pieces on the floor.

"Shit," I repeated, moving automatically to the bottom desk drawer.

I looked at Merle.

I didn't have the heart to tell her the bottle of Scotch was gone.

After gathering up the contents of my wallet, I realized nothing was missing but two Andy Jacksons and my assortment of business cards—"Nell Fury," as well as "Susan North" and a few other fabricated identities. Huh. Had my mystery assailant known who I was before treating me to an early evening nap?

I decided not to call the cops. Too invasive, not to mention fruitless. Merle didn't object very strenuously. I eyed her surreptitiously and wondered again what she meant by "talent."

One thing was certain: Merle had a gift for housekeeping. She helped me with a preliminary tidy-up of the office, attacking the room with the energy of a whirling dervish. Working more slowly, I couldn't tell what, if anything, had been stolen—except the Black Label, of course. My trusty typewriter was intact; my telephone still in service. My tape deck appeared untrammeled. I popped in an old Joan Jett just to make sure. *Yeah.* I danced around for a minute, but I had to stop because my head started kick-boxing in protest.

What had Ski Mask been after? As we righted objects and gathered fly-away papers, my memory of the attacker came into sharper focus, but I still couldn't visualize anything clearer than a hulking presence with two concave sockets for eyes. I shuffled to the door. My key was in the lock. Good. Ski Mask wasn't planning to repeat this American Gladiators escapade.

I removed the key and was attaching it to my Dollywood keychain when I noticed a piece of paper wedged beneath the threshold. It was yellow carbon, crumpled and smudged. I bent to retrieve it, smoothing it as best I could. The paper was so dirty and torn I could barely make out the purple type and accompanying scrawl of handwriting. "Look at this," I called to Merle.

She materialized at my side, dabbing a tissue against her moist brow. "Whew," she whistled, "it's hot in here."

I handed her the scrap. Merle squinted. "Looks like a bootprint, see? The waffle pattern."

"Mm-hmm."

"Must have been caught in the guy's shoe."

I looked at her with new appreciation. "Or the gal's."

"Right." Merle wrinkled her nose. "Can you read it?"

Both of us studied the carbon for a while, rotating it to check out various angles. I made out "San Francisco." Big help. Also a series of dates that corresponded with the coming week. There was a jagged, unreadable signature and a list that seemed to include the words "shovel" and "solvent."

Things were just starting to click when Merle beat me to

the punch. "It's a work order! Somebody's job assignment. And look—" She aimed a nail at a purple smear. "Doesn't that say 'cemetery'?"

"Uh-huh. And there're only two cemeteries in the city. Mission Dolores and—"

Merle piped up. "—the Presidio."

"The Presidio," I echoed softly. I carefully removed my glasses and rubbed each eye with a balled fist. Oh, lord. What can of worms had I sprung open this time?

I felt like hugging Merle. I did, spontaneously, then thought of deputizing her, too, on the spot. Which brought Darnelle Comey to mind.

"Oh, no!" I groaned.

"What's wrong?"

"I just remembered, I had a date tonight."

"Oh-h-h." Merle gave me a big-sisterly pat. "Well call him, he'll understand."

"Uh, it's a her," I said.

Merle put a hand on her hip and nodded sagely. "Ahh."

"I mean, it wasn't that kind of a date, it was business," I blustered unaccountably. It's weird, no matter how many times you come out of the closet, each new episode carries a little tinge of danger.

"Hey, it's cool, I've been around the block, know what I mean?" Merle stuck the phone in my hand. "Call her, already."

I looked up Darnelle's home number in my card file. It took longer than usual because Ski Mask had played a game of 52 pick-up with the contents. While searching through the shuffled cards, I asked Merle about the leafy monstrosity in the corner.

"It's a *Ficus elastica*," she beamed. "A rubber tree. The super let me move it in. Do ya like it?"

I chuckled. That Merle. Finally, I found Darnelle Comey's number, dialed, and got a taped greeting. Maybe she was asleep. Maybe she was annoyed with me and not answering the phone. I called my home machine to see if she'd left a message. Boy, oh boy. Had she ever. Three of 'em, in fact.

In the first message, she wondered why I was late. In the second, she was irritated I'd stood her up for Fritos and tomato sandwiches.

The third message was the zinger: "Nell, where *are* you?! It's Darnelle. Oh god, I don't know what's going on. Will you call me, puh-leeze?! Peko Muncie's been killed!"

11

I reached Darnelle at the offices of E-Z Investigative Services, where the body of E-Z top banana Peko Muncie had been found at 9:42 p.m.

I had to sweet-talk a patrol officer to get Darnelle on the line. She said the place was crawling with cops as well as most of the E-Z operatives and support staff. Nobody knew what to make of Muncie's death. He'd suffered three gunshot wounds to the chest; any one of them would have been enough.

I apologized to Darnelle and told her I'd explain my delinquency another time. Meanwhile, could she meet me someplace to discuss Peko Muncie?

"Now?!" Darnelle squealed.

"Yeah, can you get away?"

"Uhhh, I don't think so. They haven't questioned me yet—"
Big sigh. "But if it's that important, I'll think of some excuse.
Why don't you meet me out front? We can chat for a few
minutes."

"I'm on my way."

"Do you remember the address?"

"Oui, ma petite."

"Oh, Nell." Darnelle's voice quivered.

"Hang tough. I'll be there."

Merle offered to drive me downtown, but I said no
thanks. I was feeling clearheaded, unnaturally wide awake. As
Merle and I parted outside, I realized I'd never asked what she
was doing at her office so late on a Saturday night. I watched
her climb into a shiny Jeep Wagoneer and head north, fading
from sight like Glinda, the good witch, taillights turning to
little red pinpricks as she mounted the rise of Taylor Street.

Now, as I traversed the potholes and streetcar tracks on
Market Street, I wondered if my assault could have any rela-
tion to Muncie's murder. The timing was a neat coincidence.
But Ski Mask favored fists, and whoever did Muncie had used
firepower. My attacker appeared to work at—or at least have a
connection to—the Presidio. And Peko Muncie's killer? I
drummed my fingertips on the steering wheel and tried to
remember something that was tickling the corners of my
brain.

I rolled by the intersection of Powell and Market, still
teeming with street performers, kids, tourists, and folks with
no place else to sleep. It hit me. Toxic waste. Both Kent
Kishida and Peko Muncie had attended community meetings
about the problem. Now they were both dead.

Darnelle was standing beneath a streetlight, huddled in a
quilted down jacket more appropriate for an Arctic expedi-
tion than winter in San Francisco. She looked awfully cute,
though, with her single blond braid poking out from beneath

an upturned felt hat. I pulled to the curb and pushed open the passenger-side door.

"Helluva jacket, Darnelle. What'dja do? Remodel a sleeping bag?"

Ignoring my comment, she slid into the bucket seat and turned to face me. In the dim glow of the interior car light, Darnelle's soupy green eyes streaked with red looked kind of Christmasy. "Hey," she marveled, "you got glasses!"

I fingered them delicately. "Quite the intellectual, eh?"

She shook her head, lowered her peepers, and started crying. I leaned over to kiss her cheek. "Hey, I'm sorry. Close the door, I want to get us off the main drag."

I rolled around the corner, found another headless meter, and cut the engine. In this concrete jungle section of the city, the few pedestrians still out after midnight paid us no mind. I took Darnelle's hand. She fiddled with the leather edge of a cut-off finger. "Cool gloves," she sniffled.

"Thanks. So. What's going on?"

"I didn't even *like* Muncie," she blurted. "Nobody did. It's just so stressful. The cops think one of us might have done it—you know, one of the investigators. There's always so much dissension among the staff." Darnelle looked out her side window, then pivoted back to face me. "It's horrible. I was gonna quit anyway, after six more months, and go for my solo license. Now everything's screwed up."

"Maybe someone at E-Z did kill him. Do you think that's possible?"

"No! Nobody liked him, but nobody'd kill him, either."

Don't be so sure, I thought silently. Out loud I said: "Any other obvious suspects? An angry client, maybe? Somebody Muncie put away?"

"We haven't had time to talk about it, really. The cops separated us to take statements. I told 'em I was just going to the bathroom. I only have a few minutes," she added nervously, pushing back a mountain of down to check her watch.

I squeezed her hand. "Okay, I won't keep you. But listen, the reason I invited you over for dinner tonight was to ask you about Muncie."

Darnelle's pea-green eyes grew wider.

"I know, it's weird. I wanted to find out if you knew anything about a case he was working on—an undercover job. Spying on a group called Neighborhood Toxic Waste Alert."

Darnelle tilted her head and frowned.

"Doesn't sound familiar?"

"No-o-o. I've heard of NTWA, though. I read about it in the paper. But I didn't know E-Z had a case involving them."

"Hunh. Don't you guys have staff meetings? Keep tabs on each other's cases?"

"Uh-huh." She nodded. "At least, the five of us—the investigators—we report to Muncie. And he tells us what *he's* working on. But who knows? Muncie's the boss. Maybe he keeps—kept—a few things under wraps."

"Apparently."

Darnelle shifted in her seat. "I gotta go—"

"Yeah, yeah. Look, Darnelle, I know this is asking a lot, with the police around and everything, but maybe you could keep your eyes open for information about NTWA—Muncie's case file, notes, anything."

"What's this about, Nell?"

"I'm not sure," I said honestly. "But if you find anything, will you let me know?"

"Okay, but . . . maybe *you* should talk to Homicide."

"Maybe. I want to check on a few things first."

Darnelle shot me a level gaze, eyes finally lighting on the damaged side of my head. "Hey!" She practically impaled herself on the stick shift trying to get a better look. "What happened?!"

I pushed her away. "It's nothing. I got . . . punched, that's all."

"Nellie—"

"Didn't you say you had to go?"

"But—"

"Hey, chill out." I gripped the wheel at ten and two. "And about your p.i. license—you just need six more months' experience to qualify?"

She nodded.

"I'll talk to Tad Greenblatt. Maybe he can get you on at Continent West."

"Oh, Nell. Thanks!"

I knew Darnelle had a little crush on Tad, and I didn't want to encourage any more rampant heterosexuality, but I figured she deserved a break. As for Continent West—they always needed decent help.

"Okay, kiddo, scram."

Darnelle beamed, lowered her chin, and offered a hangdog grin in lieu of a goodbye. Then she hopped out and careened around the corner, her puffy coat enveloping her like a giant swirl of pale cotton candy.

It was 1:15 a.m. and I still had boundless energy. I spotted a pay phone across the street, so I darted over to disturb Lydia Luchetti's beauty rest. She'd gotten me into this thing, after all. At least in part.

I dropped two bits and turned my collar up to block the wind. Damn—it *was* cold out here.

"Hullo?" came Luchetti's groggy voice.

"Hi there. It's me, your worst nightmare."

"Nell?"

"Yours truly. Are you awake?"

Lydia sighed. Then she chuckled. "Can this wait? I—"

"I found out something about Peko Muncie."

"Oh yeah?" The journalist in her perked right up.

"Yeah. He's dead."

"What?!"

"He was murdered at his office tonight. They found the body just before ten o'clock."

"Jesus. I gotta call the *Chron*. I'll call you right back—"

"Whoa, hold on. I'm at a pay phone—"

"What's the number?"

I reeled off seven digits.

"Okay. Sit tight." Click.

I replaced the handset and stood bouncing from foot to foot. Brrrr. The wind whipping against my bruise felt like the sting of a million needle pricks. My stomach started growling. Here in the deserted urban canyons, the noise sounded louder than an eighteen-wheeler rumbling on the interstate. Yikes—when was the last time I'd eaten?

The phone jangled. "Lydia?"

"Yeah. The night desk sent some kid to cover the murder. I'm gonna go down there, but can I meet with you first?"

"Sure. I can swing by your place."

"No!" she stage-whispered. "Meg's here."

"Oh. Ummm, I'm really hungry. How about that restaurant on Van Ness—"

"Nellie, I don't have time to make a party out of this."

I bit back a retort. I was, after all, doing her a favor. A soak in the bathtub and a nice tomato sandwich was starting to sound good about now. Hell, I had all the fixings at home . . .

"The 24-hour Cala," Lydia was babbling. "You know, the one near my house. Nell? Nell?! Are you there?"

"Yeah. You want to meet at a grocery store?"

"You wanted food, right? We can talk there—it'll be quick."

I guffawed, suddenly exhausted. "You're a piece of work, Luchetti."

"What? What'd I do?"

"Nothing. Cala it is. The one at California and Hyde."

"Yup."

"See you in ten."

"Right-o."

When Luchetti arrived at the Cala, I was aimlessly pushing a shopping cart, eyes glazed, trying to decide between deli potato salad and hummus with pita bread. She took over cart-pushing while I ate a few bites of each. The potato salad was infinitely better. I wedged the whole half-pint and chased it with a carton of lemonade.

We probably looked a little odd, even for an all-night supermarket: a ravenous woman with a head injury and a pert professional type clutching a reporter's notebook. Luchetti kept tossing stuff into the cart to keep things on the up-and-up. I opened a pack of Nutter Butters and started munching.

Lydia didn't even notice my wound. Good—I was in no mood to explain. She asked about Peko Muncie and I told her what I knew, which wasn't much. This annoyed Luchetti, who was under the impression I already had info on the NTWA spy caper.

"Not yet," I explained.

"Well, what are we doing here?" she fumed.

"It was your idea, sweetheart." I chewed another cookie.

I was too fatigued to broach my suspicion about a Kent Kishida/Peko Muncie connection. But I did ask Luchetti if she had garnered any more dirt about the City's pending SLAPP suits.

"Nope," she answered dispiritedly.

I told Lydia she should head for E-Z and we could talk again in a day or two. She sighed, apologized for her short temper, and gave me one of her now-trademark puppy dog looks. Then she was out the door.

Always a friend of labor, I cruised the aisles returning

grocery items so the night clerks—hunkered over a game of five-card stud at the meat counter—wouldn't have to do it. Before exiting, I paid for my purloined snacks with an ATM card, picked up some extra cash, and, at the last minute, bought a bottle of Scotch. Out in the parking lot, the Datsun coughed, shuddered, and died with a tremulous wheeze. I turned the key again. I heard a series of clicks, then nothing. Oh, no.

I couldn't deal with this, not tonight. I tried one more time. Still nothing. I left the rattletrap under the bright orangish lights of the Cala lot and hoofed it, bottle in hand, a few blocks over to Polk Street.

A Barbary Coast cab slowed, gobbled me up, and deposited me on Ramona Avenue. I didn't bother with a bath after all. I fell straight into the sheets and reached for *The House of Real Love*. I only made it through two paragraphs. The book slipped to the floor and I was down for the count, socked into a blank, dreamless oblivion.

12

The sound came from far away, the distant peal of a church bell, perhaps, or the clang of a cable car gliding effortlessly down to the Bay. I rolled over, envisioning antique trolleys riding unbelievably steep embankments, while blankets of wispy fog and crystalline blue skies formed a picture-postcard backdrop. I shifted and the sleeves of my sweater tangled even further with the bedsheets, catching my arm in an awkward vise. A disembodied ski mask with haunted eyes drifted into my dim consciousness. I twitched. The bell droned on and on, cruelly persistent.

The doorbell. Shit. I sat up and instinctively drew a hand to the back of my neck. Everything was blurry—my head, my eyesight, the wash of gray-black raindrops against the attic window. The bedside clock read 8:45. The bell was as maddening as a ticklish cough that refused to go away.

I loped to the bathroom to pee and brush my teeth. Then I found my glasses and pushed the button to release the downstairs gate. Leaving the chain lock in place, I opened my door two inches and listened as a steady tread of footsteps climbed to the third floor. My Louisville Slugger was in easy reach.

A woman came into view. She was short, husky, and unsmiling, dressed in a creamy, dark green leather jacket and a plain black skirt. She wore nylons and flats, too. She was striding toward me brandishing a silver badge in a black leather flipcase. She held it front and center, arm rigid in front of her, like Jonathan Harker fending off Count Dracula.

"Police," she commanded. "Got a minute?"

"Uh, it's kind of early–"

"On the contrary, it's almost nine o'clock. You *are* Nell Fury?"

"Yes."

"I'm Elvia Penayo," she said to my eyeball. "You may remember talking to me?"

What a card. I sighed, removed the chain lock, and opened the door a full two feet. "Look, I'm not at my best. Can we make an appointment for later?"

Unexpectedly, Penayo grinned. She had dimples as deep as the Grand Canyon and eyes the color of newly minted copper pennies. It was a lovely combination, but I wasn't fooled. I grinned in return and held my ground.

"I'm dying for a cup of coffee," Penayo teased.

"Oh, what, now this is a social call?" I bantered back, leaning my hip against the door frame.

Penayo shrugged, flipping her leather case open and shut.

Geez, Fury, what are you doing? Flirting with a cop?!

I tossed my head and beckoned her inside. Penayo's smile vanished. She walked into the apartment, eyes darting in all directions. I'd forgotten to feed Flannery and Carson the night before so I threw them some fish flakes and retreated to the kitchenette. I was back in short order, two mugs of coffee in tow. "If you want cream or sugar, they're on the counter," I said inhospitably.

Elvia Penayo took her time with the extras, then settled next to me on the couch. "Out late last night, were you?"

I sipped some joe and mumbled, "Mmm-mm."

"Your personal life doesn't concern me, Ms. Fury. Nor your work life, for that matter, unless you tread on our turf—"

"Nell."

"What?" she said sharply.

"Call me Nell."

"Nell-l-l-l. Isn't that sweet?" Penayo's dimples were impossibly symmetrical. "What were you doing last night at 608 Market Street?"

I choked, spilling a splash of coffee on the couch. I dabbed it with the cuff of my beleaguered sweater. Damn. How did she know I was there?

Penayo pressed on, "You had a meeting of the minds with a Darnelle Comey of E-Z Investigative Services. Care to share?"

I set the mug on the table and dragged my palms down the thighs of my pants. "Darnelle and I are friends from way back, Inspector. She just needed a little consoling, that's all."

"'Consoling'? From what I hear, she didn't even like Peko Muncie."

"Uh-huh."

"So—?"

"Uhh, what I meant was, Darnelle needed professional advice. From a fellow private investigator."

Elvia Penayo lost it. She roared, snorting with deep raspy laughter. It got so bad she had to put her coffee down and unzip her jacket for air. Her eyes teared up, her laughter turned to honks.

I said dryly: "Cool it, Inspector. You'll wake the neighbors."

Penayo stopped instantaneously. Amazing. "Look," she said, "we had a man on the street last night. He saw Comey get into a car. He checked the plates and gave me the info. I ran it and—bingo!—Nell Fury. The same Nell Fury I talked to less than twenty-four hours ago about an entirely different matter." Penayo smiled. "So here I am, making your day."

"Any suspects on Muncie?"

Penayo stopped smiling.

"How about Kishida?"

She continued her impersonation of a Buckingham Palace guard. I matched her, freeze-frame for freeze-frame. We could have stayed there all day, daring each other to blink, had I not developed a killer itch. I scratched it, grinned, and said, "Aw shucks, Inspector. As I told you before, we're after the same thing here." I didn't know if that was true or not, but I decided to throw her a bone. "Ever hear of Neighborhood Toxic Waste Alert?"

She stiffened.

"I think Peko Muncie may have rubbed someone the wrong way. Just like Kent Kishida." I put my hand to my ear and cupped it, exaggeratedly. "Now, don't you hear the taxpayers calling?"

Elvia Penayo looked at me, copper eyes shining with unreadable emotion. She surprised me with a handshake, then stood and departed without looking back, dark hair bouncing rhythmically against her shoulders. I blew some air out and sank deeper into the couch. Penayo had never even tasted her coffee.

What *did* Muncie and Kishida have to do with each other? I thought about it as I showered, dabbed hydrogen pyroxide on my wound, and pulled my hair back with a scarf to let the area breathe. Muncie had tried to infiltrate NTWA; was Kishida also a part of that group? Was the City really spying on

NTWA, or had Muncie been hired by somebody else? And what about the Presidio watchdog group that Kishida was involved with? Maybe that was another organization the City was targeting for a SLAPP . . .

Or maybe the murders were totally unrelated.

I found my favorite pair of jeans in a clump on the floor. They were clean enough, though, so I pulled them on, along with a white button-down shirt and a pale-brown, oversized sweater. I opted for my old cordovan ankle-high boots with the little silver buckles. Then I tossed back a couple of extra-strength painkillers to prepare for a rash of phone calls. Ready for action.

I tried Carmelinda Kishida. Again, no answer. I called the Department of Engineering and Housing at the Presidio and asked for Rory Rafferty. She wasn't in. I punched Darnelle Comey's number. Busy signal. I paced for three minutes and tried again. Still busy.

I balanced the receiver in the crook of my neck. Hmm. What was the name of Kishida's friend on the Presidio grounds crew? It was one of those verb names: Skip, Chuck, Lance . . . Trip! Trip Hamm.

I rummaged in my coat pocket and found the scrap of paper with Hamm's number. This time I struck pay dirt.

"Hello?"

"May I speak with Trip Hamm, please."

"You've got him."

I introduced myself—the real me, that is—and said I wanted to talk about Kent Kishida. The request was met with a resounding silence.

"Hello?" I finally said.

"You're a private eye?"

"That's right."

"Kent's dead."

"Well that's just it, isn't it?"

Trip Hamm was having no part of it. "Look, Kent's murder

is old news. I'm sorry he died, he was my buddy, but the police already wrote it off as a random mugging. It's over."

"You talked with the cops?"

"No," he admitted sullenly.

"No?"

"No," he snapped. "N-O."

"But you were his closest friend at work, right? Didn't they—"

"I said no! Forget it—"

"Wait." I tried to think fast, but none of this was making sense. I quickly said, "Let me give you my number in case you change your mind. You can always call—"

He hung up.

I depressed the button slowly, watching the rain run in steady rivulets down my slanted window. The single pane of glass looked like a modernist collage-in-progress, a messy canvas of gray-streaked malaise. I released the button and called Bartholomew Lane. He answered on the first ring. "Yes?"

"Laney, hi, it's Nell Fury."

"Hello." His greeting was a wispy crackle over the wire. "I was going to call you today. How are you?"

"Okay. And you?"

"I'm tired."

We listened to each other breathe for a moment. He broke the melancholy silence with a distasteful joke, something about lawyers.

I didn't laugh. But I said, "Can I do anything for you, Laney?"

"Oh, heavens, no. But tell me, what have you found out about Kent?"

I launched into a recap of the last few days, including Charley Canton's story, Elvia Penayo's intransigence, my visit to the Presidio, and my Saturday night run-in with muscle. "Oh, dear!" Laney exclaimed at that point. I didn't tell him about Peko Muncie's murder because the connection was still so speculative. But I asked if he'd ever heard Kent mention a group called Neighborhood Toxic Waste Alert.

"Kent . . . no. I've heard of it, though. I read about it in the Sunday paper. A nice idea, very grassroots." Wow—everyone but me was up on current events these days. Laney went on: "But remember what I told you? Kent was pretty secretive those last few months. Do you think he was going to NTWA meetings?"

"Could be. I'll try to find out. Laney?"

"Hmm?"

"Did Kent ever talk about a friend from work named Trip Hamm?"

"Sure. I met him—nice kid."

"He wouldn't talk to me. Just now, on the phone."

"Oh yeah? Well, Tripp was kind of shy, if I remember correctly." Laney made a noise halfway between a grunt and a chuckle. "He and Kent used to hit the bars together. A good-looking pair, those two."

"Is that right?" I filed the comment away for later. "By the way, has Kent's mother contacted you again?"

"Yes—that's what I was going to tell you. She called late last night."

"Really?" I sat up straight.

"Um-hmm. It was odd. She wasn't angry this time, she apologized and said she hadn't burned everything after all . . . she said something like, 'It doesn't matter anymore.' Then she started talking in Spanish and I couldn't follow . . . " Laney paused. "I tried to get her to explain, but that was it. She hung up."

"You still don't know what she's talking about?"

"I can't imagine."

"I'm going to drive down there today," I said impulsively, deciding on the spot. "The address you gave me—is that still correct?"

"I think so, but if she won't cooperate on the phone—"

"I know." I tapped my heel restlessly. I needed to push a little harder, find a crack in this jigsaw puzzle. A visit with Carmelinda Kishida seemed like the logical next step. I added mischievously, "I have my ways."

Bartholomew Lane wasn't amused. "You be careful now, won't you?" He sighed noisily. "You know what? If you can't find Mrs. Kishida at home, you might try the Family Giant cannery on the outskirts of Watsonville. She works there, or used to."

"Thanks."

Laney and I agreed to meet on Wednesday, three days hence, to reassess the case. He was paid up through then. If necessary, we could extend the arrangement.

I was halfway down the stairs before I remembered my stranded vehicle. Damn. I kicked the baseboard and trotted back up to call Phoebe Grahame. Johnnie Blue answered and told me Phoebe had already left for the track.

"Argghhh," I said.

Johnnie laughed. "What's up?"

"I was hoping to borrow her car."

"Ohhh. She took it to Bay Meadows. A sloppy day out there."

"No kidding."

"What's wrong with *your* dashing roadster?"

"Don't ask."

"Ha. I tell you what—I'm not using the Acura. Wanna borrow that?"

I blinked. Phoebe's ancient Plymouth Duster was one thing, but Johnnie's precious sportscar? "Are you sure?"

"Yeah, why not? I won't need it 'til tomorrow. You can bring it back then. I just had it tuned, though, and it's still at the shop. You'll have to pick it up in West Portal."

"No problem," I said, high-fiving the air.

"I'll call and tell 'em to give you the key." Johnnie gave me directions to the service station.

Yee haw. On the road again.

13

Actually, hours passed before I hit the road to Watsonville. First I was sidelined by yesterday's mail, a haul that yielded two fundraising appeals, three advertising circulars, one bill, *Bomb* magazine, my "Investigators R Us" membership newsletter, a postcard from Harry Fury, and–gulp–a letter from Tammie Rae Tinkers.

I huddled under the archway of my apartment building and tore the flap, withdrawing two pages of computer-generated type. Rae wrote about a snowstorm, a night at the Grand Ole Opry, a dicey engineering problem, and a convention in Southern dining she thought I'd enjoy: Meat 'n' Three. You pick one meat plus three vegetables, pile on some biscuits, and call it a meal. I smiled. Then I flicked a few stray raindrops from the letter and scanned it once more, this time reading between the lines. I still couldn't find any mention of lust, love, or heartache, just the sane, practical meanderings of a contented mind.

I fought back a lump in my throat and restashed the whole wad of mail in the mailbox. Then I scurried over to Market Street to snare a taxi.

My next delay was a detour to the library to read Luchetti's infamous article about Neighborhood Toxic Waste Alert—I didn't want to be the only one still in the dark. The article was classic Luchetti: concise, serious, and laced with barely-suppressed editorial outrage.

According to my friend the ace reporter, NTWA was a confrontational new group that modeled its tactics on street-wise organizations like ACT-UP and the Women's Action Coalition. NTWA had yet to stage its first direct action. Members were researching toxic-waste dangers in the Bay Area, organizing like-minded souls around the city and gearing up for a public demonstration in the next month or two. Luchetti didn't mention the possibility of a SLAPP attack or any other action to counter NTWA's strategy. She did, however, list companies and institutions bent out of shape by the nascent environmental group, including chemical, ship-ping, mining, and multimedia interests. And the United States military.

Hmm. I made note of some names. Among the NTWA activists was a park ranger, Serita Dodd, and a novelist, David Paige. Also Christopher Mason, a name I remembered from my dinner with Luchetti—he was the man who had tipped her off to Peko Muncie. The only person quoted from the pro-business side was a woman from an international cargo company. Pamela Konstantine. I closed up my little spiral notebook, returned the *Chronicle* to its stack, and headed back into the January drizzle. It was 12:45 p.m.

I figured the underground Muni would get me to West Portal as fast as even the craziest cabbie, so I descended into the subterranean maze and caught an outbound train. West

Portal was on the far side of Twin Peaks, only one stop from the Castro, but it felt like another universe entirely. When I emerged, I was in a cozy middle-class hamlet of neat homes and time-worn establishments, a neighborhood hunkered quietly into the hillside, oblivious to the winds of change. I usually come here for action movies at the Empire Cinema, followed by drinks at the bare-boned Philosopher's Club. Now, I alighted from the streetcar and rounded a corner off the main drag. The auto shop was one block up, just where Johnnie said it would be.

I slogged through puddles shiny with oil and into the grimy front office. When I asked for Johnnie's Acura, a lad in coveralls pointed at the metallic gray beauty hoisted on a lift, poised primly like an insect caught on a stick pin. "Twenty minutes," said the lad.

"What?" I asked unnecessarily.

"Sorry, lady, we couldn't get to it before."

Damn. Would I ever make it to Watsonville? I thought of bagging the whole thing, then remembered it was Sunday. I figured I had a better chance of finding Mrs. Kishida today, while my local inquiries would fare better during the work week. What was another twenty minutes in this cock-eyed day of diversions?

I retraced my steps to the commercial strip. My boots were soggy, my head yammering for caffeine. I hugged the wall and tried to sniff out a coffee joint. On my left, I passed an Irish pub and a stationery store, then a familiar window display of coffee beans and high-tech gizmos. What do you know—a Cuppa? franchise in West Portal. That meant the Gap, Ben & Jerry's, and a Barnes & Noble superstore were not far behind.

I snickered and ducked into the storefront. Might as well tick off another perfunctory spy job.

Something was wrong. For starters, I was the sole customer. A drone of music that sounded like chainsaws crossed with a martial arts demonstration replaced the usual lull of classical lite. The countertop was littered with beans. Strangest of all, no one badgered me with a question. Behind the counter, a woman sat on a chair—another no-no—flipping pages of a book called *The Neo-Beat Omnibus*. She looked up at me with waifish eyes, two caramel-colored saucers ringed with deep symmetrical shadows. Then she burst into tears.

"Hey," I said.

Raccoon Eyes kept sobbing. I stubbed my toe against the floor and waited. "Hey-y-y," I repeated, more gently. The tears streaked her face, a glistening wash of imperceptible anguish. I noticed a pinprick mole on her right cheek, the fullness of her lips, improbably dainty silver hoops in one ear. Raccoon Eyes had fine tawny hair, short like a schoolboy's, and pale, pale skin. She might have been all of twenty-two, but I wouldn't stake my license on it.

Cuppa? management would love this; they'd post bulletins, issue directives, lower the axe. But they weren't going to find out about it. Not from me.

I glanced over my shoulder and hastily flipped the front door latch, then pulled down the burlap window shade. The store darkened. It felt every bit as dreary as the wintery gloom out on West Portal Avenue. I ducked under the counter, found the radio, and lowered the volume. As background noise, the industrial music was an almost welcome cacaphony, a life-affirming outpouring of angsty dissonance. Beside me, Raccoon Eyes swallowed tears and gazed at me with quiet curiosity. Then she reached out a smallish hand and touched the sore spot behind my ear.

It was so unexpected I jerked backwards, then stopped, staring at her wet, puffy face. She touched me again, drawing a slow, tender finger from the nape of my neck to my collarbone. My knees buckled. She wasn't crying anymore, but her eyes still shone with distress, and something else too. Determination, perhaps. I hadn't thought so at first, but I suddenly found her unbearably stunning. We traded smiles. I touched the knuckle of my forefinger to her cheek and she turned and bit it, just like that.

Beneath her mocha-colored apron, Raccoon Eyes wore a plain white T-shirt, hacked off at the sleeves. I reached under the apron strap to cup her shoulder. Her skin felt warm and sweaty. The room was thick with the scent of coffee, but I imagined other smells as well: rosemary, yeast, mud, sex. It was overwhelming, this unspoken pull, this sudden desire. I tasted salt when she kissed me, and sweetness too, a trace of vanilla. Raccoon Eyes had my coat off and was tugging at my sweater, running two hands across my back with endearing confidence.

I laughed nervously, then let it all go, thoughts of work, of Rae, of this young woman's unexplained sorrow. I pressed her against the counter and lifted her apron, unfastened the zipper of her pants. She wore nothing underneath. I heard her breath catch as I slipped a hand inside the cloth and traced the outline of her hipbone. Then I took my time kissing the area where blond fuzz ran like an arrow from her navel to her pubic hair.

We finished undressing each other there, behind the Cuppa? counter, cracks of light around the burlap shade casting angular shadows across our bodies. Raccoon Eyes guided me to a tiny storage room at the back of the shop. I couldn't remember the last time I'd had sex without conversation. My new friend rooted through her belongings and found a black velvet bag. It was startlingly sexy the way she produced her stash of latex and lube, smoothly, assuredly, as if it were a silver cigarette case or a tube of lipstick.

I could barely stand anymore, but that didn't matter, because she had me on my back in mere moments, sprawled on a mound of coarse coffee bean bags that shifted beneath me like grainy sand on a hot beach. Her eyes were bigger then ever, her smile a gentle dare. She straddled me, legs wide enough to reveal a skeleton key tattooed on her inner thigh. Then I was drowning in wet tongue, sweat, coffee, cum, a raunchy swoon of sensation and sin. When we were finished, I kissed her tattoo, her breasts, her face still blotchy with tears. She gazed back with solemn eyes and a trace of bravado, enough to send aftershocks tripping down my vaginal walls. I loved her fiercely then, in that fragile moment.

Raccoon Eyes fixed me a cup of French roast to go. I sipped it as I walked to the gas station, rain plastering my face with cold droplets, my fingertips smelling of a tryst. I could honestly report that the West Portal Cuppa? made delicious coffee. If asked, I could say the service wasn't bad either.

14

It was after four o'clock by the time I cruised into Watsonville. The light was fading, the sky a gunmetal gray behind the dense rise of the Santa Cruz Mountains. Traffic had been surprisingly heavy coming down Highway 280 and over 17. Perhaps coastal mudslides had forced travelers to the inland roads. I'd stopped for a BLT outside Capitola, fighting exhaustion with food, a jumbo root beer, and memories of a dreamy episode already etched in my brain like sepia film footage caught in a perpetual loop.

Back on the highway, Johnnie Blue's car was a mean driving machine. Her small but impressive music collection included old Etta James, new Tanita Tikaram, and my favorite Replacements tape. I'd listened to "Skyway" over and over again, trying for the hundredth time to decipher the lyrics. Failing yet again, I'd opted for silence, struggling to concentrate on the task at hand. I'd already decided to give Carmelinda Kishida my real name and occupation—I hoped to lure an explanation from her with genuine sympathy. But I wasn't sure what I could offer in return.

Watsonville was a small farming community north of the Monterey peninsula. I'd never been in the town proper, but I knew it was one of many agricultural areas in central California beset by poverty and high unemployment. When the Loma Prieta earthquake hit in October 1989, Watsonville took an especially wicked jolt. Driving into town along the main thoroughfare, I spied dilapidated structures, overgrown lots, vast expanses of open space, and a few lit-up businesses. There were no obvious signs of rejuvenation, little evidence that the town had bounced back from the quake—or would anytime soon.

The rain had subsided; there was still enough daylight to read the road signs. I relied on a rudimentary map to find Kishida's street, mysteriously labeled River Drive. There was no river in sight, unless you counted the fingers of muddy sludge that lay stagnant in the deeply rutted road.

I turned and drove along slowly, scanning the houses. When I realized there were no identifying numbers, I stopped to quiz a couple of kids immersed in a messy game of kickball. My pidgin Spanish did the trick—I asked for Carmelinda Kishida and they pointed to a house down the street with an open-air carport and a rusty swingset out front.

I pulled into Kishida's driveway and sat for a moment, finalizing my approach. Then I walked to the door and rang the bell. No answer. I tried the side door, adjacent to the carport. Again no answer. I repeated this brilliant strategy, front door, side door, front door, side door, then walked all around the house. I couldn't see a single light on inside, nor could I see anything else of particular note. The shades at the side door were drawn. An old Chevy Nova sat under the carport, gathering rust.

Dang. I yanked off my glasses and rubbed my eyes, drew my coat up tight below my chin. I was woozy with fatigue, aggravated by the relentless damp chill of the early dusk. Behind me, the sporty Acura loomed in Kishida's driveway like an alien spaceship, vibrating with temptation: heat, music, escape.

I kicked myself. What was I thinking? I couldn't give up yet. Mrs. K. could be anywhere—dinner, a friend's house, a poker game. I knew nothing about her . . . except that she worked at the Family Giant cannery. Might as well give it a try. If she wasn't there, I'd check back here in another hour or two.

An old man at an all-night mini-mart told me how to find the food-processing plant. Yes, he said, it operated around the clock, 365 days a year. Following his directions, I found the tell-tale chainlink fence enclosing the cannery parking lot. The entrance was open. I rolled past a peeling wooden sign that announced, "Family Giant: Good Foods for Good Families." Four artichokes were painted below the logo, anthropomorphized into mom, dad, son, and daughter. The woman/girl artichokes were appropriately identified with hairbows. Thank god—wouldn't want to eat the wrong gender.

Half the security lights were burned out. Most of the lot was empty. Well, maybe production slowed down in the winter. I parked beside a pink VW bug and entered through a steel door marked *"Trabajadores."* No one tried to stop me. A small office to the right of the entrance was unoccupied. It was sweltering inside, so I took off my coat and walked purposefully to the end of a long corridor. I was in a vast, low-ceilinged room crammed with vats, assembly lines, pipes, and crates. Considering its magnitude, the area was rather quiet.

A few workers gave me the once-over, but nobody said anything. I approached a middle-aged woman who was perusing a jumbled bulletin board. She didn't speak English; my Spanish didn't suffice this time. So the woman fetched another employee who bustled over and glowered at me through blue-tinted bifocals. I said hello and asked for Carmelinda Kishida.

"What do you want with her?" demanded Blue Lenses.

"Uh—" I was a bit dumbfounded by the animosity. Might as well be straightforward. "I want to talk to her about her son."

She tilted her head. "You're not with Family Giant?"

"No." I glanced around and realized half the cannery workers were staring at us.

"Ahhh." Blue Lenses clucked her tongue and patted me on the shoulder. "I'm sorry, honey. We see a *gringa* on the floor, especially on the weekend, and—" She drew a finger across her throat.

"You mean . . ." I couldn't finish the sentence.

Blue Lenses smiled sideways and eyeballed me from head to toe, like I was hopelessly bourgeoise. "Yes, honey, lay-offs. We're already down two-thirds and they're gonna cut even more. It's only a matter of time before we're all canned." She seemed to get a perverse kick out of her little pun.

I smiled weakly.

She went on: "They opened a *maquiladora* in Salvatierra, a small town near Mexico City. Shipped almost all our work down there. They pay 'em less for a whole day than we get for an hour—and that's no great shakes to begin with. They don't have to pay benefits in Mexico, either, and they just dump all kinds of crap into the rivers—"

"And things will get worse with NAFTA," I inserted.

Blue Lenses cocked her head. "You already know about this stuff?"

"Some." I knew that the North American Free Trade Agreement would be disastrous for labor both here and across the border, and that the environment would suffer, too. "I didn't know Family Giant was such a monster."

She shook her head disgustedly.

"Well . . ." I faltered, suddenly tongue-tied.

Blue Lenses let me off the hook. She asked, "What did you want with Carmelinda?"

I told my new friend about my mission. She peered at me sagely. "Yes," she finally said, "Carmelinda's been upset lately. Tell you what"—she took my arm and steered me toward the exit— "I'm just getting off work. Why don't I take you by 'Linda's house? She's like a sister to me. Maybe I can break the ice."

I thanked her and waited while she punched a clock and said a round of goodbyes. As we walked to the parking lot, she told me to call her Daisy. I never learned the rest of her name.

Daisy's truck was on the fritz so she rode with me back to Carmelinda's. Along the way, she gossiped wildly about the Kishida family, including Carmelinda's relatives in Guadalajara. It was a juicy saga full of birth, death, resurrections, marriages, funerals, graduations, miracles, and more. From Daisy's lips, it was magic realism come to life. I was exhausted just listening to her talk.

It was a remarkably fruitful car ride, all things considered. Among other salient facts, I learned that young Carmelinda Lopez had married a Japanese-American man, Yuchi Kishida, born at the World War II internment camp at Manzanar, California. Yuchi's father had enlisted in the U.S. Army and been killed overseas in 1944. Yuchi never got over his anger at the family's detainment, even though he'd been too young to remember Manzanar. In 1988, when the U.S. government offered restitution to survivors of the Japanese internment camps, Yuchi Kishida was denied the nominal sum because his father had left the camp voluntarily to join the military. This glitch in the rules infuriated Yuchi, but rather than rebel, he turned his rage inward and killed himself.

Carmelinda, in turn, had never really recovered from her husband's suicide. Then her only son, Kent—named after that hyper-Anglicized superhero, Clark Kent—had told his mother he was gay. Carmelinda was shamed even further by the revelation. But in the wake of the earthquake, the drought, and threats of a lay-off at work, Carmelinda had come around and was seeking a reconciliation with her son. Then Kent Kishida was murdered.

Daisy fell silent and stared ahead into the blackness.

"Jesus, that's awful," I mumbled. "So the rest of Carmelinda's family lives in Mexico?"

She nodded.

"How long have you known Carmelinda?"

"Fifteen years, since the cannery opened. It was a good job back then." Daisy paused before adding absently, "Kent was a sweet little boy."

I maneuvered over the bumpy stretch of River Drive and pulled in behind the Nova. There were still no lights on at Carmelinda's house. I opened the car door and turned to say something to Daisy. In the yellow haze of the Acura's indoor light, her profile looked pinched. Reflections bounced off her blue-tinted glasses like the erratic code of a distress signal. She said, "Something's wrong. 'Linda always took her car. If she was home, there'd be lights on."

Daisy was out of the car and running to the side door. I jogged behind her, watching as she dug a key out of an inside jacket pocket. She called Carmelinda's name as she jammed the key in the lock, turned the handle, and pushed the door inward. I heard the gentle bump of shades against the door window, then an unmistakable wail. Over Daisy's shoulder, through the semi-darkness, I saw a hulking shadow dangling from a rope, a strangely still bundle of clothed flesh and bone that used to be a human being.

I gagged, stumbled back against the carport.

I'd bet the farm it was Carmelinda Kishida, following in her husband's footsteps.

15

By the time local authorities sent me packing, rain was again falling from the jet-black sky in a soft, steady patter. I drove slowly over Hecker Pass, bright lights illuminating the tight curves of the roadway. I found a terrific blues station on the radio, but I was afraid I'd doze off, so I switched to lite rock, "all the soft classics of the '80s and '90s." Big mistake. After Billy Joel, Michael Bolton, and Mariah Carey, I clicked off the radio and listened to the lonely thwack-thwack-thwack of the windshield wiper blades. Much better.

No one had any doubt that Carmelinda Kishida had hung herself. All the evidence pointed to suicide. Even I couldn't dispute it, much as I would have liked to pin the blame on Kent's attacker, nail the sucker, and tie it all up with a bow. I told the county sheriff about Kent Kishida's unsolved murder up in San Francisco. He found it interesting but irrelevant. He was much more impressed by Carmelinda's suicide note, her obvious grief over her husband and son, and the termination notice from Family Giant that lay front and center on the kitchen table.

There were other documents on display as well, which I perused while waiting for help to arrive. There was a packet of letters from Kent to his mother, all dated during the summer before his death. Kent had apparently sought a mother-son reconciliation, too; the letters discussed his sexuality, his choices, and his life in San Francisco with frankness and warmth. Even more interesting were reminiscences about his father and questions about the grandfather he never knew. And then there was the part about the Presidio.

At his job, Kent wrote, he learned the Presidio was the military site from which internment orders were issued to Japanese-Americans during World War II. He said he was livid about the country's ongoing denial of the travesty and—specifically—the Presidio's lack of public acknowledgment of its role. Kent told his mom he was meeting with a park ranger to discuss the issue. He hoped to persuade the National Park Service to be more forthcoming and historically accurate about the Japanese concentration camps when the Presidio became a part of its domain.

So, further evidence that Kent Kishida had been a budding activist. I wondered if the meeting with the park ranger had happened before he died. And if the two incidents were at all related.

There was another manila envelope on Carmelinda's kitchen table; this one was a dandy. Inside the well-thumbed package was a short stack of hate mail, single-paged notes addressed to Kent that dripped anti-gay venom. Racial epithets, too. The notes were made of colored construction paper and individual letters cut out of magazines. It was a kindergarten project from hell, masterminded by someone who'd watched too many episodes of Perry Mason. The notes might be comical if the sentiment wasn't so dead-on vicious.

Each piece of paper had a thumbtack hole at the top. Somebody had pinned up these little valentines for Kent Kishida to see. I felt sickened. And more certain than ever that Kishida's killing was no random affair.

There were seven notes total. I slipped one inside my coat pocket. Local law enforcement would surely take a gander at these items, but I wanted one for safekeeping, in case no one else took them seriously. I had a hunch these were the papers Carmelinda Kishida had initially claimed to burn. I'd never know for sure. I wondered why Carmelinda had fixated on Laney; maybe he was the only one of Kent's friends she'd ever met—maybe she knew something I didn't know. But from what Daisy had said, Carmelinda must have been agitated by this display of hate directed at her son, one more stroke of devastation in her troubled life.

Fleetingly, I wondered if she'd found the notes in Kent's apartment and, if so, how the cops had overlooked them. Perhaps Kent had simply mailed them to her. I double-checked the manila envelope. It was unmarked.

Daisy hadn't minded my quick scan of the evidence. For one thing, she was too overcome to worry about me. Besides, she seemed to think it was part of my job. When the law arrived, Daisy was composed enough to explain why she and I were in Carmelinda Kishida's kitchen on that fateful evening. Later, Daisy gave me a tearful goodbye hug under shelter of the carport, as emergency vehicles clustered in the driveway cast a dizzying wash of multihued lights across the small wet yard. Reflected in Daisy's shell-shocked eyes, I swore I saw an image of her friend's lifeless body.

The image continued to torment me as I powered north. I was nearing the city limits of San Jose when I realized I wouldn't make it home that night. The streetlights were a blur of shimmering white glitter, my eyes a couple of slugs, heavy with lethargy. Dammit, Fury, you're losing your stamina. I veered down an exit ramp and forced myself to sit upright, scanning the frontage road for motel signs. I was out of my league here—the vast sprawl of San Jose was still a mystery to me.

I rolled slowly past apartment complexes, flat-roofed businesses, a massive construction site that had to be the future arena of the new expansion hockey team, the San Jose Sharks. So far, Sharks merchandising had been way more successful than the team itself. Ah, the wonders of advertising. Phoebe had given me a teal-and-black T-shirt that featured a monster shark chomping through a hockey stick. Loved it.

I kept driving aimlessly, passing rows of spindly palms that shot into the night sky like fireworks caught in mid-burst. The rain fell insistently. I realized I was in the middle of town; I'd circled twice around the same city park. I felt crazy tired, a bundle of frantic exhaustion. Finally, I stopped at a well-lit oasis with a Roman-style sign out front that read "Cafe Leviticus." The joint had the spacious look of a bank metamorphosed into a hipster hangout. I sleepwalked to a teller window where a bald grrrl with crimson lipstick served up coffee in a bowl and directions to Motel 6.

I would've hugged her, if not for the daunting marble slab between us. Instead, I drained half the coffee and hightailed it to the motel. Orange carpet and a velvet clown painting had never looked so good.

Sure enough, as soon as I slid between the cotton-poly sheets I was wide awake. I couldn't staunch the questions darting around in my head like panicky mosquitoes in a bug net. I shuffled over to turn on the TV. There was Barbara Stanwyck in full cowboy drag, stomping around a dusty corral. Perfect: an old western called *The Furies.*

I lay back on the lumpy pillow to watch Stanwyck lock horns with her cattle rancher father. Next thing I knew, the

TV was a bright splash of morning newsclips and talking heads. I rolled over and groaned. A blade of white light fell across the motel bed like a portentous wakeup call from the heavens.

16

The sun hung low in the sky when I ventured outside to find a convenience store. I bought a toothbrush, shampoo, cranberry juice, and a package of Fig Newtons. Back in the room, I showered and washed my hair, paying special attention to my dinged-up scalp. It seemed to be healing, though my moppish hairdo was still a bit of a hindrance. I brushed it back with my fingers, threw on the same old clothes, and had a little snack. My watch hands were parked at 7:45.

Apparently, Motel 6 didn't provide complimentary stationery, so I dug out my pocket-sized spiral notebook to use instead. I sat crosslegged on the bed and made a list. Once I got back to the city, I'd cancel my lunch date with Charley and Dawn. It was a shame, but somehow I wasn't in the mood anymore—at least not today. Then I'd call Johnnie and arrange to return her car, as planned. Maybe check in with Phoebe, too. And I supposed I'd better call the Cala and see what they'd done with my hapless set of wheels.

Afterwards, I'd head for the office. I wanted to talk to the following people, in no special order: Darnelle Comey, Rory Rafferty, Trip Hamm, if he'd deal with me, any of the people from NTWA, somebody from the National Park Service, and my client, Bartholomew Lane. Whew. Depending on how things went, maybe I'd turn the whole ball of wax over to Elvia Penayo, along with the purloined piece of hate mail in case she needed a little extra persuasion.

I drew a flower-power daisy in the margin of my notepad. Then I made a row of question marks at the bottom of the page and drew arrows from item to item as if I were Ross Perot discoursing on economics. My diagrams made about as much sense as his. I frowned, and tried flipping the notebook open and shut as if I were Penayo playing tough cop with her badge. It was a bust.

I gathered my meager belongings and trundled out to the Acura. Rush-hour traffic was already waning on the Bayshore Freeway. I cruised, making one brief stop along the way at a Cuppa? in Redwood City. Duty called. I got my house blend in a to-go cup and was back on the road, steaming northward to patch up the pieces of my frazzled life.

Dawn answered when I called the Cumberland Street residence. I remembered her voice from the first time I'd phoned. Now she was sweet. She oozed understanding and suggested we reschedule for later in the week. I felt oddly ambivalent, but couldn't come up with a ready excuse, so Charley, Dawn, and I were on again for Thursday lunch at Elka. I scratched my head and dialed the Twin Peaks retro-pad. Yes, Phoebe would drive over in about an hour to pick the car up. We signed off. I riffled through the White Pages and found the number for the Hyde Street Cala. That's when I hit the first glitch of the day.

"You have no record of it?" I asked blankly.

"That's right, ma'am."

I was talking to a Cala manager who checked the log books and told me no Datsun B210 had been towed from the Cala lot on Saturday night or Sunday.

"Well then, it's gotta be in the parking lot," I insisted. "It's kind of beat-up looking. It's, uh . . . brown."

"Ma'am, I sent a bagboy out there. No Datsuns at all. Any color."

"That's just not possible. Perhaps you'll go check yourself?"

I had to admire the guy's patience. We'd already been over the same ground twice. The manager just let out a steady breath and said, "One moment, ma'am." I waited. He was back in three minutes. "No Datsun B210," he reported smugly.

Weird. I got him to give me the number for the towing company. I suppose whoever yanked the car could have screwed up the paperwork. But when I called Toe-the-Line Towing, they also claimed to have no knowledge of a dead Datsun at the all-night Cala. They promised to scour their lot, though, and call me if they found the vehicle.

I decided not to worry about it for the time being. I freshened up and went hunting for a clean outfit. I found dusty-blue trousers, a favorite T-shirt faded to robin's egg blue, and a smoky-blue Father Knows Best cardigan. Hmm. Well, I'd read monochromatic was all the rage. Look out, fashion world.

I still had half an hour to spare so I got back on the line and called London. Pinky was out, but her other mom, Caroline Zule, answered the phone. Caroline and I had been lovers in the old days, when Pinky was an infant and lesbianism was racy and clandestine, not stylish. Now the two of us shared custody and an easy—if distant—rapport. Caroline told me Pinky was leaning toward returning to the States after high school. Then she dropped a bombshell.

"She wants to find her father," Caroline said.

"What?!"

"I know. After all this time."

Pinky's father had walked out on me when I was five months pregnant. He'd never met his daughter, nor even inquired about her. I'd met Caroline soon thereafter and instantly realized what I'd been missing: women. I harbored no grudge against the old boyfriend. I didn't mind Pinky's interest in her dad, either, not theoretically. It was just so sudden.

"Eddie Meadows," I said, as if in a trance.

"That's the guy." Caroline's voice was sullen.

"Has she tried to contact him yet?"

"No. But she said she's picked up enough tips from *you* to know how to find a missing person—"

"*Car*-o-line—"

"I'm sorry," she said unconvincingly. "Look, we probably shouldn't sweat it. She's almost an adult. It's not like we have to worry about custody or anything."

"Umm."

"I think Pinky's developed a romantic notion about her father's life. Now that she's considering her own choices, her urban experiences may seem limiting . . ." Caroline rattled on in professorial psychospeak, one of her least attractive tendencies. I listened patiently, but part of me was thinking about Eddie Meadows, a poet-dreamer type who used to want to be Sam Shepard. Last I heard, he was working at a cattle ranch in Wyoming. Pinky knew that, too. No wonder she harbored romanticized ideas about him—I wouldn't mind running off to Wyoming, either.

I cut into Caroline's monologue. "Hey, I gotta go. Thanks for the news. Will you have Pinky call me?"

"Of course. Nell, did she tell you she won a poetry contest sponsored by the London *Times*? Best emerging poet under eighteen. They published 'Road Kill.' Isn't that great?"

"The best," I replied.

I was still beaming when Phoebe and Johnnie showed up to reclaim the Acura. Johnnie had to split, but Phoebe hung out for a while and asked me about my bashed head, my visit to the Presidio, and my trip to Watsonville. Suddenly, I was overwhelmed with gratitude for Phoebe's attentiveness. I jumped up and kissed her on the cheek. She batted me away playfully and said, "Nell, I don't suppose you can get a look at the police report? About Kishida's murder?"

"No, probably not."

Phoebe knew I was generally on the outs with the S.F.P.D. Tad Greenblatt can pull that kind of magic, but not me. I'm sure he'd help me out on this one, except he'd left another message on my phone machine—he had decided to extend his vacation. Tad would be out of town the rest of the week. The nerve.

"Too bad," Phoebe said when I told her. "Maybe the cops know something they're not letting on. Something obvious—"

"Are you talking cover-up?"

Phoebe hunched her shoulders.

"Maybe, Phoebes, but it seems more like plain old negligence to me. Kent Kishida was gay, working-class, a person of color . . . not your priority murder victim."

"Yeah."

Phoebe and I stared at each other. Out of the blue she asked, "What's your client's name again?"

"Bartholomew Lane. Why?"

"You said he had a crush on the kid. Maybe *he* killed Kishida and hired you to hide—"

"No." I shook my head. I couldn't believe that.

Phoebe eyed me pensively. "What about the mom? Maybe she did it and couldn't stand the guilt anymore—"

"No, no, no." There *must* be something obvious I hadn't yet grasped, but I didn't think it involved Carmelinda or Laney. I had a nagging sense it had something to do with Kishida's attendance at town meetings and/or NTWA. But I couldn't figure out how. What had Charley Canton overheard? Two fleeing assailants and the word "mace" or "maze." There was no indication Kishida had fought back with mace. Maze? What did that mean?

Phoebe cocked her head and said, "Okay. But you shouldn't be so cavalier about getting beat up the other night."

"Cavalier, *moi?*"

Phoebe feigned a jab to my gut. "Nellie, somebody's on to you. From what you told me, somebody from the Presidio."

"I know. That's good. If I keep up the pressure, whoever it is is bound to trip up."

"Nell Fury, robo-dyke."

"*Phoebes.*"

"Just be careful, Fury."

"You bet."

Phoebe tooled off to the airfield. She had a few more routine lessons to complete before conquering her maiden solo flight. I went down to the basement storage room. If the Datsun hadn't surfaced in a day or two, I'd look into renting a car. Meanwhile, my old Schwinn ten-speed would tide me over. As long as the weather held, anyway.

I found the two-wheeled dinosaur in more or less working order. The tiger-striped paint job was as dazzling as ever, its tattered leather seat still molded to perfection. I filled the tires with a hand pump and went back upstairs to fetch the brown leather jacket with the fake fur collar that Rae had left behind. I tugged on my fingerless gloves. Just right for a winter ride.

It was almost noon when I pedaled away down Ramona Avenue, feeling the brisk slap of wind in my face and the splatter of mud flying up from the spokes. Nature: I could never get enough of it.

17

My office was still in mild disarray, but the rubber tree, with its brilliant waxy leaves, looked healthier than ever. I smiled and opened the blinds to let in as much light as possible. I perched on the edge of my easy chair and hit the play button on the answering machine.

There were several generic inquiries about private eye services, a friendly "How's it going?" from my sister Grace, and a couple of clicks. I could return most of the calls later. The only message of immediate concern was from Darnelle, who said "Call me!" in that eager-beaver voice of hers. I complied. I found her at home, not at the office.

"Nell! I—"

"Hiya, Darnelle."

"—I got the file!"

I punched the seat cushion beside me. "Nice going. What—"

"You were right!" Darnelle panted. "Peko Muncie was working for the City. The D.A.'s office hired him to get information about that group you mentioned—Neighborhood Toxic Waste Alert. He was supposed to figure out who the key players were, their strategies, targets, stuff like that. I've got—"

"Darnelle, was it Margaret Halliway?"

"What do you mean?"

"The client. Was she the person who hired Muncie?"

"Oh. Let me see . . . ." Darnelle hummed a riff as she checked the paperwork. It sounded like old Elton John, maybe "Benny and the Jets." Darnelle came back on the line. "Halliway . . . she's the district attorney, right?"

"Um-hmm."

"Nope, it wasn't her. It's a guy—Conrad Smith. You know him?"

"No. Is he an assistant D.A.?"

"Uhhhh, yeah. That's what it says."

I rubbed my palm over the worn leather armrest. It felt buttery and smooth. "Do the cops know about this?"

"Yeah, they sure do. They took all of Muncie's current case files." Darnelle Comey explained that she'd gone to E-Z Investigative Services late last night, figured out Muncie's computer access code, and printed out another copy of his NTWA file. "So I've got the official records, but none of his handwritten notes," she added mournfully.

"Can I see what you *do* have?"

"Sure!"

"Thanks, you're a champ."

Darnelle said she was heading downtown later today. I gave her directions to the office, and told her to slip the file under the door if I wasn't in. I hadn't told Darnelle about the Kent Kishida case, so I didn't bother reiterating the saga about Carmelinda's suicide. But I still had that hunch that Muncie's murder was related to Kishida's. I asked Darnelle if the police had any theories about Muncie.

She sighed. "That's the thing. Muncie had so many enemies, they suspect everybody. His ex-wife, his old business partner, his secretary. Geez. Not me, thank god. Even though they put me through the wringer."

"What's happening at E-Z?"

"I don't really know. The cops still have the place cordoned off. All our work is on hold."

"Well, Tad Greenblatt is still out of town, but as soon as he's back, I'll try to fix you guys up." I laughed. "As co-workers, I mean."

"Oh, *Nell*."

After a profusion of thank-yous, we rang off. I called Lydia Luchetti at the *Chronicle*, got her voice mail, and passed on the information that Muncie was indeed spying for the City. Hopefully, it would give her a new burst of inspiration for her investigative series. Afterwards, I found my little spiral notebook and double-checked my rambling notes from this morning. Better call Laney.

When I did, I got his answering machine. Damn. I didn't want to leave the news of Carmelinda's death, so I just told him to get in touch. Then, just as I began to look up NTWA names in the phone book, my unlisted telephone rang.

"Hello?" I answered nonchalantly.

"Susan North, please."

"Speaking."

"Ms. North, this is Rory Rafferty from the Presidio Department of Engineering and Housing. I understand you wanted to talk with me about Kent Kishida?"

"Why, yes," I said, struggling to remember my ruse. "I'm developing a television docudrama about—"

"I can spare twenty minutes. Today, fifteen hundred hours. At my office."

Aye aye, I wisecracked inwardly. But I simply said, "Fine. Three o'clock."

I replaced the receiver. Yikes—this was Kent's friend?

I finished my search for NTWA names. Serita Dodd was listed so I wrote down her number. No David or D. Paige. Plenty of C. Masons, though. I scribbled all the possibilities, then picked up the phone and called 411. Neighborhood Toxic Waste Alert had a listing.

I called and got a taped hotline. The message recited current toxic waste emergencies in the Bay Area and what citizens could do to combat them. A few examples: plumes of sulfuric acid hovering near the Richmond oil refineries, illegal dumping of hazardous waste in a Hunter's Point landfill, the contamination of the San Francisco Bay with plastics tossed off naval carriers. I felt increasingly queasy as the hotline droned on.

The phone message encouraged people to call or write various legislators, CEOs, and media outlets. It also mentioned different groups working together with NTWA— labor unions, public health organizations, community groups, Silicon Valley environmentalists, a military base conversion/ clean-up project. Wow. NTWA may be a band of young, feisty upstarts, but they sure knew a thing or two about coalition-building.

I was impressed, and also exhausted thinking about it all. At the end of the message, NTWA encouraged everyone to participate in the group's first mass action, scheduled for late January at the Presidio's abandoned Nike missile site. According to NTWA, the Presidio was awash with contamination problems, from underground storage tanks to asbestos in post buildings to a proliferation of pesticides and medical waste.

Kent Kishida's boss, Stu Clemens, had said the same thing, only he implied the problem was under control. Furthermore, I hadn't known NTWA had targeted the

Presidio as a top priority. Huh. The Presidio was popping up everywhere. I stood up and peered through the blinds. My pigeon friends were back on the neighboring rooftop, happily scavenging for morsels during this respite from the rain.

Suddenly starving, I wandered next door to see if Merle wanted to join me for a bite. There was no answer when I knocked. Rats. I checked my watch. I could either initiate another round of phone calls, or treat myself to lunch before meeting with Rory Rafferty. It was an easy decision.

I left the Schwinn in the office and rode the elevator to street level. I was getting fond of my little stretch of Taylor Street: the Muffin Coffee Shop, the Art Theatre, a corner bar called the 65 Club that beckoned with decadent promise. I kept walking, and wound up at Original Joe's for a plate of spaghetti. On the way back, I spotted the sign for "Precision Haircuts." Hey—might as well take the plunge.

"Precision" was definitely a misnomer. I asked the woman to snip around the sore spot. She took me literally, cutting a donut-like swatch of topiary behind my left ear and hacking the other side in an artful attempt at symmetry. She cut the bangs like an inverted picket fence, and left a stray hank in the back poking out in a single flippy curl. I practiced smiling in the beauty shop mirror. It required a great deal of will power.

I tipped her hastily and fled across the street, where I engineered a quick repair job in the fifth floor bathroom. Now I looked like a little kid with a bowl cut and her first pair of glasses. To hell with it.

I threw some water on my face and ran my gloved fingers through the short crop. Then I grabbed the bicycle and lit out for the streets.

18

I had to walk the steepest block of Leavenworth Street, but after that it was a daredevilish coast from Nob Hill to Fisherman's Wharf. I felt warm in my leather flight jacket, the wind a welcome tease around my newly exposed neck. I hung a left at Chestnut Street, dodged a mammoth tour bus, and followed the straight, flat road into the pristine Marina district.

If private-eye work grew stale, I could always become a bike messenger, I thought, in a moment of temporary insanity. Then I nearly got creamed by a speeding Ferrari. Better put that idea on the back burner. Entering the Presidio, I was again struck by the instant transformation from urban streets to dense, exclusive parkland. I was a bit turned around, but I spotted familiar landmarks and followed my instincts. I arrived at the Department of Engineering and Housing with ten minutes to spare.

I locked the Schwinn to a rusty anchor that apparently marked the site of some historic conquest. The orange tiger stripes added a nice touch of modernity. I paused to cool down, taking in the magnificent sweep of Presidio trees and the breathtaking hills of Marin. Because of recent rains, everything appeared more lushly green than usual. The DEH building, in contrast, was a lump of concrete the color of wet oatmeal.

My meeting with Rory Rafferty was almost a complete waste of energy. Clearly, she'd decided ahead of time to blow me off. Whether it was disdain for Hollywood or complicity in Kishida's murder, I couldn't be sure. I also wondered if she knew I was a private investigator—whoever ransacked my office had ascertained that Susan North and Nell Fury were one and the same person. If Rafferty knew, we were both pulling off a stunted bit of playacting.

Rafferty was pushing forty, a clean-cut, plain-faced woman with pale-blue eyes, flawless white skin, and an outfit so crisp it looked like it would cause bruising if you got too close. Her manner was off-putting as well. Again, I wondered why she and Kishida had been friends. Well, there was one possibility, I thought, tuning into my lesbian radar. Hmm. I couldn't tell. If Rafferty was a dyke, she had burrowed her way deeply into the closet.

I did learn that Rafferty was a mid-level administrator for the DEH, and one of the military personnel who would be relocated when the Presidio became a part of the National Park Service. I could tell she wasn't happy about it. In terms of her friendship with Kishida, she would only admit that they had shared occasional cocktails after work. His murder was a tragedy, she said, but she had no reason to think it was anything but random. Turning his story into a TV docudrama would be pure exploitation.

I asked Rafferty if Kishida ever talked about environmental concerns or the Presidio's involvement in the internment of Japanese-Americans. I watched her lips tighten and her eyes narrow into icy blue marbles. She simply said no, and dismissed me with a haughty wave.

Before departing, I managed to garner one potentially useful bit of info from this tedious exchange: the combination to unlock a vertical storage unit in her office. The opportunity came when she took a phone call and had to pull a file from the metal cabinet. Over her shoulder, my spectacles gave me an eagle-eye view as she twirled the cylinder of the dime store lock. 36-16-8. My age, Pinky's age, my shoe size. Piece of cake.

I pedaled away from the DEH, wondering if I should try to track down Trip Hamm again and see if I could get him to talk. Might as well, but first I needed a bathroom and something to quench my thirst. I rolled over the smooth Presidio roadway, pondering whether or not mere civilians were allowed to use the Officer's Club. Probably not. I was starting to feel desperate when I spied a familiar logo plastered discreetly on the side of a stucco building. Burger King! I'll be darned. And it even had a bike rack out front.

I locked up the Schwinn and moseyed inside, noting the huge arched windows framing Doyle Drive and the twin spans of the Golden Gate Bridge. This was the swankiest Burger King I'd ever seen: ceiling fans, stained wood booths, a trillion-dollar view. I used the bathroom and was waiting in line for a root beer when I heard a recognizable voice coming from behind a frosted glass partition. I quietly ordered a large soda, took my cup, slunk around the corner, and slid unobtrusively into a booth on the other side of Stuart Clemens, head honcho of Kent Kishida's maintenance crew.

". . . I heard the old lady offed herself," Clemens was saying.

"No shit," responded a second voice. "That's weird."

"Damn, I hope she didn't have the notes," Clemens whispered, clearly agitated.

"Don't worry about it. Why would *she* have them? The kid probably ripped 'em up."

"I don't know. He was turning into such a little prick. I'm afraid he might have been saving them, to try and sue us or something."

"Fuckin' fags," seethed Voice #2.

"Cool it, Dickie, until this thing blows over—"

"Yeah, yeah."

Dickie?! I chortled into my drinking straw, my mind racing to connect the dotted lines. Apparently Clemens and his pal Dickie had sent Kent Kishida those juvenile pieces of hate mail. To try and scare him away from his job, I imagine. And now Clemens was worried somebody might find the notes. Did that mean he and Dickie had killed Kishida?

"I wish I could be sure," Clemens went on. "You're positive they weren't at that lady's office?"

"Yup."

"Run it by me again. You followed her, like I told you to, and she ended up on Taylor Street . . ."

I choked on a swig of root beer and tried to muffle my tortured cough. *Dickie* was my attacker, the person in the ski mask! Damn. I felt like strangling him, but I forced myself to stay cool.

". . . and you checked through *all* her stuff?"

Dickie sighed in annoyance. "Jesus, Clemens, how many times do I have to tell you? She's a private dick, she's working on Kishida's murder, and she didn't have the notes. I don't think she even knows about them—"

"Dickie—"

"—and even if she does, so what? *We* didn't kill the kid."

"But if they find the notes, they'll think we did," Clemens blustered. "She's stirring it all up again!"

Aha. Clemens sicced his underling on me to find out if I was being straight with him. And if I knew anything. I was glad I'd nabbed one piece of the evidence—maybe it would be enough proof to cause these scumbags some grief. Meanwhile, I wondered if they knew who really murdered Kishida. I decided to dog them for a while. Maybe they'd spill another juicy revelation. I'd have to look for Trip Hamm another time.

I arched my back against the stiff wooden bench. Clemens and Dickie had moved on to work-related topics. Clemens mentioned some rigamarole about Army-Park Service cooperation. Dickie grunted. Then they discussed an afternoon project—apparently they had to go check the parade grounds and something called the Agave Path. Sounded familiar. And scenic. I'd just follow along, a silent shadow to their every move.

I realized my mistake as soon as they left the Burger King. I had figured Dickie and Clemens would go on foot, but when I slunk behind them into the parking lot, I saw them climb into an Army pickup truck. Uh-oh. As they sat warming the engine, I swiveled my neck in search of a solution, and found it in the form of a Yellow Cab. The driver was well into a Whopper when I yanked open the back door, dove onto the seat, and said, "Follow that truck!"

"You gotta be kidding," he mumbled around a mouthful.

I peered carefully through the side window and saw the pickup rolling slowly out of the parking lot. I fumbled through my wallet, pulled out a fistful of greenery, and waved it in the cabbie's face. "Please," I said.

"That'll do it."

My Whopper man was a wizard behind the wheel. I kept my head down and listened to the clunk-clunk-clunk of the tires as we left the Presidio grounds and headed onto regular San Francisco streets. The driver offered monosyllabic clues about our whereabouts. Lombard, Van Ness, North Point Street. Yikes. I thought they were going to the Presidio's main parade ground, just blocks from the Burger King. Another mistake. The cabbie careened to a stop.

When I poked my head up, we were in the heart of Fisherman's Wharf. Dickie and Stu had parked in a lot across from the wax museum and other fine cosmopolitan sites. The Whopper man shrugged and gently urged me to exit the vehicle. A gaggle of tourists was converging on his cab like a giant swarm of money-bearing locusts. "Thanks," I murmured, dumping my hard-earned cash in his lap.

I scurried from car to car, keeping my prey in sight. I watched them mount the wooden steps to Pier 41 and bypass a line of people slowly boarding the Alcatraz ferry. Oh, my god. There was an area on Alcatraz called the parade grounds, too. Clemens and his helpmate were going to The Rock.

I almost laughed. Was it worth the trip? What the heck. I hadn't been out there in a number of years. I used to work as a deckhand for the Red & White fleet, so I squinted through the crowd to see if I recognized any of the deckhands working today. Yup, an old pal of mine was straddling the gangplank, making sure none of the eager visitors took a tumble into the murky bay.

I waited until all the tourists had boarded, then strolled up to greet Maria. She gave me a sloppy hug and an invitation on board. Clemens and Dickie had climbed to the upper deck, so I stayed down in the cabin, chatting with Maria as the ferry chugged its way across the choppy waters.

We gossiped for a few minutes before I asked her why Army maintenance people would be working out on Alcatraz. She provided an obvious answer. Now that the Presidio was changing hands, Army expertise was being utilized all over the Golden Gate National Recreation Area, including on Alcatraz Island. According to Maria, the prison-turned-park was targeted for a lot of renovations: the cellhouse, the parade grounds, historic gardens, bird nesting areas.

"Is there something out there called the Agave Path?" I asked.

"Yup," she said. "It's a scenic trail that runs around the south side of the island."

Of course, now I remembered. The Agave Path. I thanked Maria and went to hide out in the bathroom as the ferry began its swooping approach to the Alcatraz dock.

I felt the boat bump gently into the rubber guardrails. I cracked the door of the toilet and watched as hordes of people trooped off the ferry. When I saw the maintenance men head up the gangplank, I merged with the crowd and kept them in sight. Amazingly, another whole mess of people milled around the dock, waiting to return to the mainland. I'd forgotten what a madhouse this place was. At least the sheer numbers gave me a measure of anonymity.

I checked my watch. It was a little after four. Clemens and Dickie split off from the teeming masses trudging up the hill to the prison. My guys cut left instead, ignored a large "Keep Out" sign, and headed into an area of dense brush. I was right behind them. Nobody came by in a Smokey the Bear hat to give us advice. Or to stop us.

19

Had I known I was going for a hike, I would've donned more rugged footwear. My arches hurt, my heels throbbed, and my legs were beginning to cramp by the time we completed a speed-walk around one side of the island. The Agave Path was an overgrown trail that followed the Alcatraz shoreline, leading to a spectacular view of downtown San Francisco. The sights got even more impressive as the walkway zigzagged up a slope and opened onto a litter-strewn patch of concrete. Behind us, the entire city rose up in neat geometrical blocks, strangely poignant in gloomy tones of beige, white, and gray.

I hunkered behind an abandoned box-spring mattress and watched Clemens point things out to his companion, stopping to consult a map now and then. Both men took measurements and jotted notes. The wind was whipping too fiercely to hear very much but, apparently, we'd arrived at the parade grounds and Dickie and Clemens were simply discussing clean-up plans. I was starting to have a lousy feeling about this afternoon jaunt—it seemed rather pointless. Oh, well. I lifted my fake-fur collar as a gust of January air blew in from the west.

When Dickie and Clemens disappeared into a clump of bushes on the far side of the parade grounds, I sprinted across the chipped concrete, determined to stay on their heels. Above me, tourists swarmed around the lighthouse and streamed in and out of the cellblock. The burned-out warden's house loomed disapprovingly over the spectacle, as if aching to tell real-life stories about the island's lesser-known travesties. I shivered, and continued my fleet-footed game of cat and mouse.

Dickie and Clemens emerged once more onto a public roadway, skirted another chainlink fence, and headed for the north side of the island. There were more places to hide over there: concrete bunkers, rocky ledges teeming with vegetation, crapped-out buildings.

I remembered it was the industrial section of the island, where prison inmates had operated a power plant, washed laundry, worked in factories. Most of the buildings were now empty shells. In a chilling way, they were a beautiful sight—stark urban ruins backed by turbulent, unforgiving waters and a static, deathly gray sky.

I shook myself out of my macabre reverie and trailed Clemens and Dickie into a rectangular old factory. I could follow a lot more closely here by hugging walls and keeping obstacles between us. It was finally worth it, too, because the conversation took an interesting turn. I stopped behind a rusty metal door and listened as Clemens outlined demolition plans for the industrial complex, then segued into a non sequitur about Kent Kishida and Army Intelligence.

"It would have never worked anyway," he said.

"Huh?" Dickie was distractedly rummaging through debris, making it hard to eavesdrop. Clanging, crunching, and stomping noises kept drowning out Clemens' words. Dang–I wish he'd cut it out.

"Kishida as a–CRUNCH–spy. It never–CLANG–sense," Clemens explained.

Dickie perked up. "Kishida was working for Intelligence?"

"You didn't know that?"

"Nope." Dickie resumed stomping.

"Shit, yeah, it was–CLANG–idea. The kid was into this environ–CRUNCH–garbage, so they figured he'd–SMASH–logical. Everybody needs a little extra dough, right?" SLAM. BAM. BOOM. "I gotta–CLING–windfall, it's a breeze."

"Hunh. So what was Kishida's problem?" Dickie asked.

"Besides getting himself killed?"

Dickie snickered. "Right."

"He was overly sympathetic to those fucking neighborhood matrons–"

Just then my foot slipped on a piece of broken glass, causing my shoe to slam against the half-cocked door. The metal slapped into the adjacent wall with a resounding thud. I held my breath.

Dickie said, "What was that?"

"I don't know . . ."

I heard the men clomping in my direction. Silently, I backpedaled through another doorway and crouched around a corner beneath a decrepit ledge. The underside was slick with grime. My heart clamored in my chest. Dickie and Clemens were casing all the rooms in the vicinity, but they failed to find my corner hiding place. I heard their voices fading away. From a distance, Clemens said, "Must have been the wind. Come on, let's go."

I let out a long shallow breath and sunk onto my heels. Better let them get a head start.

When I emerged from the factory, dusk was beginning to

settle over the region. Everything was blessedly quiet here, far from the buzz of the city. I couldn't remember the boat schedule, but the last ferry must be leaving soon. I hustled back along the western shoreline, then decided it'd be faster to cut through the cellhouse. I ran up the treacherous steps to the exercise yard and bounded into the prison itself.

If I remembered correctly, you could bypass an entire switchback by exiting through the shower room. I found the back stairs and tripped into the eerie depths of the Alcatraz basement. I could barely see anymore. The sickly green walls looked especially putrid in the gathering darkness. Jesus— where were the park rangers? Shouldn't they be closing up shop?

I practically flew down the sloped roadway, my oxfords slipping dangerously on their well-worn treads. From some- where behind me, the lighthouse began its hypnotic rotation. I felt skittish and wary and tried to dodge the ribbons of light, as if I were a fugitive, the real McCoy. Finally, I burst through the old covered sallyport and sprinted for the dock, just in time to see the Red & White ferry leave an oily trail of churning water in its wake as it powered away with the last load of passengers for the day.

Damn. I fought back a wave of panic, and rotated 180 degrees to take in the massive hunk of rock rising behind me. Old military barracks from the Civil War era were chopped into the hillside; scores of gaping black windows taunted me with vacant stares. To one side, a rickety guard tower stood watch over the barren Alcatraz dock. "Indian Land" was still scrawled on the front of a building, angry graffiti from one of the island's many phases of political tumult.

I bounced in place, trying to stay warm. What the heck, I thought, giving myself a little pep talk. It was wonderfully serene out here and a great place to be in the event of an earthquake. I laughed aloud, still nervous. Then I squinted, imagining the whole place as a movie set, with Clint Eastwood and Tyne Daly running roughshod over the rocky shores, and Burt Lancaster wandering placidly amid a flock of birds. Ha.

The sky was almost completely dark. A spotlight provided a brilliant splash of light across the entire dock. I headed for what looked like an office tucked into the base of the barracks. I wondered if there were phones on Alcatraz. Suddenly, I saw a flicker of movement beneath the shadowy eaves. I froze. A man walked onto the dock to greet me, as if we were casual acquaintances having a chance encounter in the neighborhood.

"Hello," he said.

"Who are you?!"

"Ralph. Security."

I gawked. He was the most benign-looking security guard I'd ever seen. He was maybe 5' 2", 100 pounds, a light-skinned Black man with gold-rimmed glasses, a matching gold front tooth, and a fringe of dreads across the front of his small head. He wore khakis, a fatigue jacket, and an A's cap turned backwards, like somebody's kid brother who had borrowed clothes a size too big.

"Security?" I repeated.

He grinned. "It's a job."

Ralph lead me into the tiny Alcatraz office where a space heater took the chill out of the air. He explained there was always one guard out here overnight, and there were almost never any problems. "Who wants to mess with this place?" he said, reasonably enough.

"Don't you get . . . scared?" I asked.

Ralph's tooth glinted. "Never."

"So," I said, suddenly sheepish, "do people miss the boat very often?"

"Nope."

Ralph was a man of few words. No wonder he liked this job. No people, no hassle. Except for the likes of me, so busy with my numbskull surveillance I'd lost track of the time. Ralph told me he could call the Coast Guard, but they would charge a hefty fee to escort me to the city. Or, he said, he'd give me a break: I could stay overnight and catch the first ferry back in the morning.

"What?!"

Ralph smiled again. I was starting to like this guy. I gave in. I didn't want to pay that fee. He guided me up a circular iron staircase to the park ranger's lounge buried in the bowels of the military barracks. There was no heat, but there were cots and plenty of Army-issue wool blankets. Ralph offered me half his supper, but I didn't want to deprive him, so I just accepted a hunk of sourdough bread. We munched companionably, listening to the screech of birds and the occasional moan of the Alcatraz foghorn. When we were finished, he showed me a stash of paperback books and bid me goodnight.

I selected a novel I'd been wanting to read for some time: *Neon Rain* by James Lee Burke. I burrowed into a cot and read for a while, but I was way too restless to concentrate, much less fall asleep. Against my better judgment, I nabbed a park service flashlight and trekked through the maze of barracks up to the top of the island. I didn't go into the cellhouse; that held no appeal. I just sat on a bench near the lighthouse, staring at the twinkling mirage of San Francisco, and thinking about Kent Kishida, his mother Carmelinda, Peko Muncie, and my client, Bartholomew Lane.

So Kishida had been working undercover for Army Intelligence. Huh. I still couldn't piece it all together. My case seemed as deliriously complicated as the bustling blur of traffic I could see darting helter-skelter along the byways of the city.

My thoughts moved on to other people: Pinky, Darnelle, Phoebe, Rae, and an enigmatic young woman with caramel-colored eyes. I remained glued to the bench until the chill penetrated clear to the bone. Then I trooped down the road, tumbled into bed, and stayed up ridiculously late reading the harrowing, evocative *Neon Rain*.

20

Ralph was as unflappable in the morning as he had been the night before. He looked rested, too, when he popped into my sleeping chambers to offer me black coffee in a tin mug. I accepted, grateful for the warm touch of metal against my icy fingers. "The first ferry arrives in twenty minutes," Ralph said, before retreating back down the circular staircase.

I found my glasses on the floor next to the cot. I put them on, yawned, and surveyed the dreary cave-like space where I'd passed the night. Wild. Pinky would love this. Maybe she'd think I was as adventurous as her vagabond father. I nabbed *Neon Rain,* stumbled down to the water's edge, and tried to freshen up in the rustic bathroom, but I still felt awfully scummy when the boat sidled up to the dock to disgorge its first round of bright-eyed visitors.

I couldn't believe it. The ferry was nearly full and it wasn't yet ten in the morning. I didn't remember it being this crowded a decade ago when I was working for Red & White. I stood there dumbfoundedly as the stream of people filed off the boat, preceded by a handful of fresh-faced park rangers in starched green-and-gray uniforms. A couple of rangers stopped to chat with Ralph, who nodded pleasantly at me before sauntering onto the ferry. I was about to follow him when I noticed the gold-plated nametag worn by one of the rangers: Serita Dodd. Whoa. My lucky day.

The deckhands were eyeing me expectantly, but I waved them off, yelled "Thanks!" to Ralph, and trotted after the tall, lean figure of Ms. Serita Dodd, Alcatraz ranger and NTWA activist. I could always catch a later ferry, but reaching Dodd by telephone wouldn't be so simple. "Excuse me!" I called out as she stepped into the little dockside office.

The woman gave me a friendly public-service smile and pointed up the hill toward the cellhouse. "No, thanks," I said, extending a hand. "Can I talk to you for a minute?"

Dodd frowned slightly, hesitating in the doorway. She finally shook my hand while glancing pointedly at her watch. "I've got a tour in twenty minutes—"

"That's fine, I'll keep it short." I found a spare business card in the bottom of my bag and passed it to Dodd. She gave it a glance, then arched one brow into an upside-down V.

"What's this about, Miz . . . Fury?"

"I saw your name in the paper, in reference to a group called Neighborhood Toxic Waste Alert. I wanted to ask you—"

"Oh, thank goodness." Serita Dodd grinned broadly, genuinely. "I thought this was gonna be about my ex-husband!"

"Heavens, no!" I exclaimed, joining her in a bawdy laugh. She didn't elaborate about the ex, and I didn't ask. She invited me into the office where the space heater was providing a modicum of relief from the elements. I sat across from Dodd, noticing her dangly silver earrings, brightly painted lips, and shiny black hair tucked beneath her broad felt hat. None of the other rangers milling around looked nearly as glamorous.

"So," she said, "what do you need to know about NTWA?"

"I'm looking into the background of a man named Kent Kishida—"

"Oh, yes." Dodd's gaze dropped to the floor.

"You knew him?"

"Mm-hm. It's so sad. Was he a friend of yours?"

"No. I'm working for someone who was, though." I shoved my hands into my pockets. "Do you know if he ever attended NTWA meetings?"

"Well, indirectly."

"What do you mean?"

"NTWA is concerned about building bridges with other community groups, not just environmentalists," Dodd explained. "So we schedule meetings with different folks in town who we hope will be our allies."

"Uh-huh," I encouraged.

"Kent came to one of those meetings. It was last fall, in the Marina. I noticed him right away because—" She laughed. "Well, because he was one of the only men."

"Was that common? To have so few men?"

"No, not at all. But this group was mostly housewives in the Marina and the Presidio Heights area."

"Oh, the watchdog group?"

"Right. They're worried about what will happen when the Park Service takes over the Presidio—like it'll become another Yosemite or something." Serita Dodd cracked up. I didn't see what was so funny. Alcatraz already felt like one of those jam-packed tourist hellholes. The Presidio might suffer the same fate.

"Anyway," she went on, "since then, NTWA has been working with the neighborhood watchdog group—they're concerned about toxic waste, too, just like us. We're trying to pressure the military to clean up the Presidio before they vacate. I'm sorry, I'm getting off track here." Dodd checked her watch. "We were talking about Kent?"

"Uh-huh. You said he was at that meeting last fall?"

"Oh yeah. I said some things during the meeting, and afterwards Kent came up to meet me. That's the other thing—he and I were the only people of color there."

I nodded.

Serita Dodd explained that when Kishida found out she was a park ranger, he had asked to get together with her to talk about Japanese internment during World War II. Dodd had been willing, but the conversation never took place. He had been killed only weeks later.

Dodd said she remembered Kishida as shy and naive, but eager. She hadn't even known he worked at the Presidio until news of his death came out in the papers. "I felt so bad," she said quietly.

I murmured understandingly.

"I'm sorry, I've gotta get to work," Dodd said. She stood and fiddled with her chin strap. "I don't suppose I've been much help."

"Sure you have. Listen, can you think of anyone who might've been pissed off because Kent attended that meeting? Or upset about his interest in the Japanese internment camps?"

Dodd gave me a funny look. "You think he was *killed* because of this stuff?"

I shrugged. It did sound pretty preposterous. But I was feeling quite certain Kishida's murder had a connection to the Presidio—someone there didn't appreciate his after-work activities. Maybe Stuart Clemens and his sidekick were guilty, after all. But Clemens had mentioned Kishida's involvement in Army Intelligence. Perhaps "maze" was a code word of some sort . . . .

134

"You should talk to Chris," Serita Dodd said briskly, breaking my concentration.

"Hmm?"

"Christopher Mason. He's in NTWA, too, one of the heavies." She grinned. "He's a good guy, though. I think he met Kent the same night I did."

Dodd quickly scrawled some figures on a scrap of paper, Mason's home and work numbers, she said. I wanted to ask her about Peko Muncie, but she waved goodbye and disappeared through an arched tunnel near the door of the office. Must be another shortcut to the Alcatraz cellblock.

I dawdled on the dock while I waited for the ferry, watching seagulls divebomb unsuspecting visitors. I felt like I'd been stranded here for days. It was nothing, I suppose, compared to how the lifers must have felt. The ride to San Francisco took ten minutes, then I killed another thirty on a bus ride to the Presidio. A fine drizzle was coating the city in a cold mist. If I didn't rescue the Schwinn, it would become permanently rusted to the Burger King bike rack.

I was a wet rag by the time I made it home to Ramona Avenue. Flannery and Carson were excited to see me—that was something. The phone machine beckoned, too, but I ignored it while I fed the fish, sorted yesterday's mail, and stripped off my muddy clothing. I turned on the radio to see if I'd missed any earthshaking news while holed up on Alcatraz. Apparently not.

I flipped to Top 40 and caught the 4 Non Blondes in the middle of a song, praying, praying *every single day* for a revolution . . . .

Yeah. I stepped into the shower and clicked on the second radio for a blast of stereo surround-sound. I watched the water pool and disappear in a clockwise, soapy swirl, and wished my sorrows could be washed away so effortlessly.

21

It was 11:30 a.m. when I settled at the counter for home-brewed coffee and an English muffin. I poured a second mug and called Toe-the-Line Towing. They still had no record of a mud-colored Datsun B210. Could someone have *stolen* the damn thing? What a strange concept.

I reached Christopher Mason at his place of business, which seemed to be some kind of direct-mail fundraising outfit. I told Mason who I was, and that I'd recently spoken with Serita Dodd. He said he'd be happy to meet with me—how about tonight after work? We agreed on the Edinburgh Castle, a drinking establishment on Geary Street, not far from his office.

So I had the rest of the day to get my affairs in order. I wanted to check the NTWA file Darnelle Comey was supposed to have dropped off. But first I checked my messages and returned a couple of personal calls. Then I tried Laney and got his answering machine. Shoot. I still hadn't talked with him about Carmelinda Kishida's suicide. I hooked my feet in the rungs of the kitchen stool and thought about what Phoebe had suggested: what if Bartholomew Lane had murdered Kent Kishida over unrequited love? *Nooo.* I felt disloyal even considering it, and resolved to swing by Laney's apartment on my way to Taylor Street.

I finally reached Pinky Fury in London. We gabbed for forty-five minutes. My heart skipped all over the map as she described her interest in the wayward Eddie Meadows. I mostly listened, though I threw in a few more plugs for San Francisco. Then I congratulated her on the publication of "Road Kill."

"Oh, Mum," Pinky said softly, her blush registering across all the miles.

I felt pretty good when we hung up. Pinky might venture off to Wyoming, but I was reasonably sure she'd come home to my beloved little metropolis when she completed that quest. I went to get dressed and realized a trip to the laundromat was in order. So I threw on sweats and the turquoise cowboy boots and trudged around the corner to Starwash. I finished *The House of Real Love*—a sure bet for my Favorite Lesbian Novels collection—as my garments suffered through the spin cycle. Then I buried myself in *Neon Rain* while the dryer lived up to its name.

It was a short hilly ride from Ramona Avenue to the corner of Diamond Street and 20th. The rain had stopped and the air felt warm and invigorating. This brief workout was a breeze compared to my dash around Alcatraz Island.

Bartholomew Lane's building looked even more chi-chi now than it had the other night: well-kempt, clean, inviting. I pressed Laney's buzzer. No answer. I peered through his bay window. No lights, no sign of action. I rang again. I was about to try another tenant's bell when I heard footsteps behind me. A large man with shaggy graying hair was climbing the stairs, arms laden with grocery bags.

I smiled. "Hi, there."

"Hi."

"Do you live here?"

"Yeah. What do you want?"

"I'm looking for Bartholomew Lane."

Shaggy Head appraised me. "You a friend?"

I nodded.

"He's away for a couple of days."

"Here, let me help you," I offered, grabbing a grocery sack before the guy could object. "Is Laney all right? I mean, health-wise?"

"Sure." Shaggy Head squinted at me as he dug a key out of his pocket. "Well, he's not great, but he's doing okay. Considering."

"So . . . he'll be back soon?"

"Yeah, he just went to the Russian River for a couple of days."

"Ahh." I fidgeted while he opened the door to the other ground floor unit. "You know, maybe you can help me."

"If it's about an apartment, there aren't any vacancies—"

"No, no." I shifted the groceries to my left hip and withdrew a fresh business card from my bag. I'd replenished my supply this morning. I handed it over and said, "It's about Kent Kishida."

Shaggy Head had bloodshot eyes that shifted from the card to me and back again. "Jesus," he said. "Come on in."

I hit the jackpot. Shaggy Head—a.k.a. Troy Stevenson—told me he saw Kent Kishida the night he was killed. Kent and two other men were leaving the apartment building when Troy got home in the evening.

"So Kishida's assailants were in his apartment!" I blurted.

"That's what it looks like," Troy concurred.

"Did you tell the cops?!"

He dumped his grocery bags on the counter and turned away.

"Well?"

"I was stinkin' drunk that night." Troy pivoted to face me. "I don't remember much."

I sighed. "But you did talk to the police?"

"Yeah, sure. I told them about the two men. But I couldn't describe 'em for the life of me."

No question, Troy Stevenson felt bad about it. I didn't want to rub it in, but I asked, "Can you remember anything at all?"

"One guy was white, the other guy Black. They were—" He scrunched up his mouth. "—regular size. Big help, huh?"

I grinned ruefully.

Troy went on: "The cops think they were a couple of bar pickups—rough trade."

"You don't agree?"

"I have no idea. God help me. I remember one other thing, though. Those two guys? They didn't seem gay."

I shot him a quizzical look.

Troy smiled apologetically. "No offense or anything, but you know what I mean—it's easy to tell. Take you, for instance. You're straight, right?"

I said goodbye. Then I coasted downhill to the Tenderloin, marveling at Troy Stevenson's bad judgment.

22

The rest of the afternoon flew by in a flurry of bureaucratic busy work. First I read Peko Muncie's file about Neighborhood Toxic Waste Alert. Unfortunately, the investigation was still in its preliminary stages. There was no *there* there, as Gertrude Stein would say—nothing I didn't already know. Except confirmation that the D.A.'s office hoped to SLAPP the renegade environmentalists for conspiracy and disruption of business advantage.

Next I pulled files on my own outstanding cases. I finalized a couple of reports and prepared packets to mail to clients. I updated the Cuppa? file, too, which required a little creative writing on the West Portal entry. Then I checked my finances. With a few large checks due in and my ongoing Cuppa? stipend, I should be okay until the end of the month. Unless I needed to buy a new car. Hmm.

One way or another, it was time to close the Kishida case and start scaring up some new business; maybe I'd return some of those inquiring phone calls. For one thing, I didn't want to keep draining Bartholomew Lane's no doubt limited resources. Besides, I felt like I was spinning my wheels. I decided to give it another day, until my scheduled meeting with Laney. Maybe Elvia Penayo would take it from there and attack the murder investigation with renewed vigor.

And maybe the Cubs had a shot at the World Series next season. Dream on, Fury.

Trip Hamm's reticence was still bugging me. Perhaps if I told him about the hate mail directed at his pal Kent Kishida, he'd be more forthcoming. I tried unsuccessfully to reach Hamm at home and at the Presidio. I left my name and number with a Presidio clerk on the off-chance he'd bother calling me back. Another long shot.

My office was still a bit discombobulated in the wake of Dickie's late-night marauding. I spent some time returning things to their usual degree of disorder, then sank into my magenta chair with my marked-up spiral notebook and a fresh pad of paper. I was once more diagramming the Kishida case, this time with a rainbow assortment of felt-tipped pens, when the telephone warbled.

"Fury Investigations."

"Nell, it's Lydia."

"Hi." I sat up and absently rubbed the shaved patch on the back of my head.

"They arrested a suspect in the Muncie murder," she said dispassionately.

"No shit." I tightened my grip on the phone. "Who is it?"

"A businessman from Memphis. Name of . . . hang on, I wrote it down." I heard her rustle some papers. "Name of DeWayne Miller."

"Well?"

I waited. Luchetti coughed. I waited some more.

"Lydia," I finally demanded, "who is he?!"

"I don't really know. He was in town on business—sales of some kind. The cops found prints in Muncie's office and matched 'em with this guy Miller, who has a prior conviction in Tennessee. Armed robbery. They found him checked into the Fairmont Hotel."

"DeWayne Miller," I mused out loud. "Did he know Muncie?"

Luchetti blew out an exasperated puff. "Nell, I haven't had a chance to look into it. The police only booked him a few minutes ago. I just thought you'd want to know."

"Hey, I'm grateful." Geez—what was her problem? I had one idea. "Are you writing it up for the *Chron*?"

"No," she seethed.

Aha. What a crack detective. "They gave it to the cub reporter?" I inquired gently.

"*Yes*. And Muncie's murder is related to my NTWA story, I just know it! Goddammit."

"Well, follow it up anyway, Lydia. You'll blow them away if you make the connection. Anything that'll sell papers."

"Harrumpphhh!"

I tucked the phone against my shoulder and steepled my fingertips. So, the *San Francisco Chronicle* didn't want Luchetti to write about the arrest of DeWayne Miller. There could be any number of reasons: to give the cub reporter more experience on the police beat, to allow Luchetti time for her feature-length articles, to avoid paying unnecessary overtime. Who knows? But it seemed odd the *Chron* would eschew Luchetti's well-regarded byline in favor of a novice for this potentially explosive story.

I snapped back to attention. "Lydia, do you know if they found the murder weapon on this DeWayne Miller?"

"I don't know. If so, they didn't release the information."

"Hunh. Maybe Miller was a client of E-Z Investigative

Services. That would explain why his fingerprints were in Muncie's office."

"Of course," Lydia said rudely. "Will you ask your friend at E-Z about it?"

"Yes, ma'am." I saluted the empty air.

"I'm sorry, Nell. It's just—" Lydia's voice cracked. "I can't . . . ohhh . . ."

She started sobbing into the telephone. Oh, dear. I made soothing noises, but nothing seemed to penetrate her weepy fog. She kept it up for a minute or two until finally, gulping, she admitted, "Meg and I had another fight. She kicked me out."

"Damn." I thought about it. "Geez, I'm sorry."

"I'll be okay, it's just . . ." Her voice trailed off.

"Do you have a place to stay?" I asked trepidatiously.

"No-o-o-o," she hiccupped, before lapsing into another long-winded crying jag.

I sighed. "You want to stay with me? My place is really small, but—"

"No, thanks," she muttered miserably. "I couldn't do that."

I let my eyes roam around my spacious fifth-floor digs. "I know. You can sleep at my new office. It's quiet here, it's private—"

"Really?"

"Sure." I looked at the old wood floor, the peeling window sill, the bird sanctuary on the roof next door. "It has all the amenities," I lied.

"Thanks!"

I told Lydia I had evening plans but she could meet me here at 9 p.m. When we hung up, I realized there was nothing for her to sleep on, unless I hauled my spare futon from home. I shook my head and walked over to Merle's.

She opened the door with practiced panache, then did a

double-take when she saw it was me. "Nell, baby, how's that head?"

I grinned and executed a 360-degree spin.

Merle gasped. She promptly whisked me down the hall to the bathroom and showed me what a little hair gel can do. I had to admit, my crop looked awfully sophisticated this way, slicked back with a discreet flip at the ends. "And it'll grow back in no time," Merle whispered.

I asked if she had a couch I could borrow. Merle looked at me sideways, then waltzed me back to her office. Huddled amidst a jungle of potted plants was a plush pink chaise lounge that would comfortably fit someone three times the size of Lydia Luchetti.

"Cool," I said.

"I'll need it back in a few days," Merle warned.

As we hefted the cumbersome chaise, I gave her office a surreptitious once-over. Aside from the tumultuous jungle effect, the room was surprisingly spare. Merle's desk was a black metal monstrosity that may well have predated the building. There was nothing on the walls. Nor any other clue about Merle's mysterious line of work.

We got the chaise into my office with a minimum of pushing and prodding. Merle collapsed onto the velvet pile with a Gloria Swanson-esque swoon. I applauded her performance, then ravaged my desk drawers looking for the fresh bottle of Scotch. I must've left it at home. Damn. When would I ever get to repay this woman for all her troubles?

Merle shrugged it off. "That's okay, Nell. I have an appointment, anyway. Gotta run." She floated out the door. "Don't do anything I wouldn't do!"

I could've sworn I heard her giggle tee-hee.

Before leaving to meet Christopher Mason, I called an associate in Memphis who used to be a private investigator. He was now in the microbrewery business, which is *not* one of the five hundred things I'd consider if I chucked the gumshoe life. But my friend knew his way around the muddy Mississippi, and he still owed me a favor. I cashed it in on a request for info on Memphis businessman DeWayne Miller.

"Right-o, Fury," said the brewery man.

I had three hours until my rendezvous with Mason. I spent two of them at the Lumiere Theatre watching a smashing little movie called *Gas Food Lodging*. It was all about love, loneliness, and the kind of work women do and get underpaid for. It featured Ione Skye, and long, slow pans of the dusty New Mexico desert. I was almost happy when I stumbled outside and walked through the early evening gloom to the Edinburgh Castle.

23

A woman with pale, stringy hair and a droopy flowered skirt was crooning a hillbilly lament when I strolled into the cavernous bar. I leaned against the vast wooden slab at one side of the room and watched a portly bartender in a stiff white apron power me up a pint of McEwan's. I thanked him, sucked foam, and asked, "Who's the singer?"

"Iris DeMent," he growled.

DeMent, DeWayne . . . what was the deal? Everyone was DeSomething all of a sudden. I slapped a DeLincoln on the bar and carried my pint to a wooden booth along the far wall.

Maybe a dozen people were watching Iris DeMent, and half of them were regulars who would've watched the Dallas Cowboy Cheerleaders without batting an eye. The Edinburgh Castle is a nice cross between a neighborhood dive and a hangout for punks, queers, and other social misfits who still enjoy a lungful of second-hand smoke with their alcohol. I eyed the Scottish coat of arms on the wall, the crossed swords displayed like trophies, and the laconic dart game underway at the back of the bar. If Christopher Mason suggested this place, he couldn't be all bad.

Another great thing about the Edinburgh Castle is the fish 'n' chips from ye olde English fast-food joint across the alley. I placed an order and settled back to listen to Iris. Hey, she could really wring the emotion out of a song. By the time Mason arrived, I was misty-eyed over DeMent's woeful country warble.

"Are you Nell Fury?" asked a loose-limbed man in an olive coat and brown plaid scarf.

"Uh-huh." I stood up.

"Chris Mason."

Mason's hand felt rough and meaty. I smiled as he sunk into the booth across from me. Mason was a rangy fellow with a reddish face, watery blue eyes, and a nervous habit of flicking his lank brown hair off his narrow forehead. He wore a suit and tie beneath his overcoat.

"Want some fish 'n' chips?" I offered congenially.

He wolfed a vinegary spear of fish, then craned his neck in search of a barman. A Scotsman appeared and took Mason's request for a Bud. Mason blew out some air, then smiled at me broadly. He looked kind of like an adult Dennis the Menace. "Sorry," he said. "It takes me a while to unwind after work."

"No problem."

We polished off the food while Mason briefly described his job at a direct-mail house. From what I could gather, he was mainly a statistician who compiled and analyzed computerized lists of donors. No wonder he was tense at the end of a workday. His beer arrived and I steered the conversation to the topic of Neighborhood Toxic Waste Alert.

"So you talked to Serita?" Mason asked.

"Yeah. She said you met Kent Kishida the same night she did?"

Mason bobbed his head and flicked his hair. "Yeah, at a meeting in the Marina. She mention that?"

"Um-hmm."

"It's a shame. He seemed like a good kid."

"Yeah? An ally?"

"Yup. Smart. Really dedicated."

"Is that right? I understood he was a newcomer to community organizing."

"Well, sure," Chris said hurriedly. Then he grinned. "But that meant he wasn't burned out yet, not like the rest of us. Kent had a lot of energy."

"Hmm. Here's the thing." I decided to be totally up-front with Mason. "I'm trying to figure out if Kishida's murder had anything to do with your group, NTWA, or with the Presidio watchdog group. Can you think of anyone who would have been threatened by Kent's actions?"

"Aside from the entire Presidio Army base?"

"Right." I guffawed and swallowed some McEwan's. "I mean, anyone in particular."

Flick, flick went Mason's hair. "I think he was killed by someone who hates homosexuals. Which certainly could mean an Army guy, maybe somebody Kent worked with."

I raised a brow.

"You said it yourself, Nell. The kid was new to Green politics. If somebody wanted to nail an environmentalist, they'd probably come after me." Mason sounded almost proud.

"Has anyone in NTWA been threatened?" I asked, trying to keep my skepticism in check.

Mason shrugged. "Not to my knowledge. But there're people out there . . . have you heard of the 'Wise Use' movement?"

"No."

"It's a coalition of rabid anti-environmentalists. They have ties to big business—lots of money, lots of corporate support. They *have* threatened community activists in other cities."

I listened as he described the alleged scare tactics used by people in the Wise Use movement. According to Mason, environmentalists had lost jobs, been run out of town, and received death threats, all so that corporate interests could maintain their profit margins at the expense of public health and natural resources. He said children were even being harassed in some communities, in order to frighten their parents. ". . . it's a desperate situation," he concluded, "that calls for an aggressive response."

Mason's blue eyes crossed a little as he picked at the label on his beer bottle. Then he surprised me by whipping out a pack of Winstons. I didn't say anything as he lit a cigarette and wrapped his arm around one knee. He smoked and said: "I got a little off-course there, didn't I?"

"Actually, it reminds me of something else I wanted to ask you about." My mind was tripping all over itself. If what Mason said was true, the Wise Use strategy had the same intent as a SLAPP suit—to stifle public outcry, albeit through slightly more extreme measures. I asked, "Did you hear that Peko Muncie was killed?"

Mason coughed. "Who?"

"Pe-ko Mun-cie," I enunciated slowly, "the guy you ratted on to the press."

"Jesus." Mason slugged his beer. "He was spying on *us*, Nell."

"I know. So now you remember?"

"Of course. I just didn't hear you."

"Ah."

"How'd you know about that? I haven't seen a story in the paper yet—"

"I know Lydia Luchetti."

"Oh."

"So," I ventured, "you know the D.A.'s office is planning to sue NTWA?"

"Yeah. I suspected as much. Just another goddamn obstacle."

Mason seemed agitated now, which made sense, I guess, under the circumstances. I asked if he'd heard about the arrest of DeWayne Miller. Mason shrugged no and mashed out the Winston. Oh, well. Time to get back to Kent Kishida.

I posed a few more questions. Yeah, Chris knew about Kishida's anger over the Japanese internment camps. No, he knew nothing about Kishida's supposed undercover work for the Army. And no, Kishida had never mentioned being hounded by anti-gay coworkers.

"But I still think he was killed by homophobes," Mason added, bringing us back to square one.

I sighed and swished around the dregs of foam at the base of my glass. Christopher Mason was making motions to leave. I thanked him for his time. As he stood to pull on his coat and scarf, he mentioned the NTWA action planned for later this month at the Presidio. "Will you come, Nell?" he asked with a shaggy-dog smile and a flick of his bangs.

"I'll keep it in mind," I said neutrally.

Mason loped away from the booth, trailing one end of his plaid scarf behind him. The wool brushed against the tabletop, sweeping something to the floor with a gentle whoosh. I bent over and retrieved a matchbook. "Hey!" I called after Mason, but he had already vanished.

I tossed the matchbook between my palms and listened to the muted crash of Led Zeppelin coming over the Edinburgh Castle jukebox. Iris DeMent must be on a break. I decided to sip another pint and wait for her second set. I had another free hour before I was due to meet Lydia.

I ordered a McEwan's and glanced idly at the matchbook. It said Rum Boogie Cafe in bright gold lettering, with yawning alligator jaws nipping at the words. Sounded like a good time.

I flipped open the matchbook cover. Inside were the initials T.F. and a scrawled phone number with a 901 area code.

Huh. 901 was vaguely familiar, but I couldn't place it. While waiting for my beer, I went to use the women's room and stopped at the pay phone on the way out. Good thing I didn't need to make a call. Somebody had cranked the jukebox to a bone-rattling volume.

I grimaced and leafed through the phone book in search of the area code map. I could never find the damn thing . . . aha! There it was. It took me a moment to scan the states and find 901. When I did, I could hear my own gulp over the din of screeching guitars.

Memphis, Tennessee was in the 901 area code.

24

Lydia Luchetti was waiting for me outside 25 Taylor Street when I arrived at 8:53 p.m. She was huddled in the urine-stained doorway with her arms crossed and one foot flat against the cement wall behind her. The street was crawling with overflow from the 65 Club, but Luchetti was in her own little daze, unaware of the riffraff milling around on the sidewalk. I brushed her cheek with a light kiss, grabbed her shoulder bag, and hustled her inside.

Lydia gave my hairdo a cursory glance, but she was apparently too miserable to needle me about it. In the elevator, a trio of tipsy men in tuxedos tried to entertain us with jokes. Lydia rolled her eyeballs as they stumbled out at the third floor landing. Good—she was coming around. When we got to the fifth floor, I showed Luchetti the pink chaise lounge, the bathroom, and the fire escape. Then I told her about Christopher Mason's matchbook.

She didn't get it at first.

"Lydia! Mason's been in Memphis. Or he's been *with* someone who's been in Memphis, like—"

"DeWayne Miller!"

"Bingo."

Luchetti whistled and started pacing. Nothing like a juicy tidbit of news to snap her out of a funk. I picked up the phone and formulated a quick ruse. Then I dialed the 901 number for T.F. that was written in Mason's matchbook.

I got a generic recording—a woman's voice asking the caller to leave a message. I hung up.

It would be eleven o'clock in Tennessee. The brewery man never went to bed early when I knew him. I punched his number and heard a voice croak, "Whaddya want?"

Oops. "Hey, sleepyhead, it's Nell Fury."

"Jesus," he grumbled, "I just talked to you a few hours ago—"

"I know. Did you get anything on Miller?"

"You're crazy, Fury."

"C'mon. You must have made a call or two—"

The brewery man dropped the telephone. I smiled and gave the thumbs-up sign to Luchetti. He was back in a moment. "Okay, let's see now. I just started this, mind you—"

"I know."

"DeWayne Miller. Born in St. Louis in '49. September third." He paused. "Miller robbed a liquor store in the early 80s. That's his only prior, in Tennessee, anyway. He kinda cleaned up his act after that. Now he's a bigshot in this association of Black business owners."

"What kind of business is he in?"

"He sells hospital equipment."

"Hunh. Anything else? Do you know what he was doing in San Francisco?"

154

"Nope. You gotta give me a chance here—"

"Let me ask you something else," I interrupted. "You ever hear of a guy in Memphis named Christopher Mason?"

"Ummm . . . nope. Kind of a common name, though."

"Yeah."

I gave the brewery man the number for T.F. and asked him to check his local criss-cross directory. He came back and told me the number belonged to someone named Felicitas Moret. He spelled it, gave me her address, and supplied me with DeWayne Miller's office address, too. He said he hadn't yet nailed down all the personal info.

"You're the best," I said. "Happy fermentation."

"Ppffff," he muttered.

When I punched the T.F. number again, just to double-check, I heard a trace of a French accent in the woman's taped message.

"Well," I said to Lydia. "Fuh-*lee*-cee-tas More-*ay*!"

"What?" she said, baffled, fastidiously dusting the leaves of the rubber tree with a square of paper towel.

"Never mind."

It was my turn to make tracks in the floor as Luchetti unfurled a cocoon-like nylon sleeping bag on the pink chaise lounge. I remembered what Laney's neighbor had told me: on the night of Kishida's murder, one of his visitors was a Black man, the other white. Luchetti interrupted my speculations to ask me for an update. I filled her in, but part of my mind was moving on, wrestling with what to do next. A telephone call took the decision out of my hands.

"Fury Investigations," I barked.

"Miz Fury?"

"Yes?"

"This is Trip Hamm."

I practically gobbled the phone in my eagerness to talk. "Hel-*looo*. What can I—"

"Ma'am, I'm really worried." Hamm's voice was low and strained.

"About—?"

"I've been getting some nasty phone calls. Real threatening. I was gonna call the police, but then I remembered how they dealt with Kishi . . ." Hamm's voice petered out.

"You mean Kent? Kishida?"

"Yeah. They sorta laughed at him."

"What do you mean? Was Kent getting calls too? Crank calls?"

"Uh-huh. For a couple of months before he died. And now, this thing that's happening to me . . ." Again, he trailed off.

"It seems similar?"

"Yes, ma'am."

"Where are you calling from?"

"Home."

So Kent had been subject to phone threats *and* hate mail. I wondered if Stu and Dickie were up to their old tricks, harassing Trip now that Kent was gone. In any case, I figured I should follow up on it. I asked Trip Hamm if I could come see him.

He said yes, and gave me an address on Larkin Street near Filbert. I told him I'd be there in half an hour. When I hung up, Luchetti was sitting cross-legged on her cascade of down and assessing me with wide troubled eyes. I suddenly felt like a heel.

I walked over and sat at the foot of the chaise. "You want to talk, Lyd? About Margaret or . . . anything?"

She worked up a smile. "Thanks, no. I was actually thinking about Christopher Mason and this guy Miller. And my NTWA story." Luchetti sighed. "But I'm so tired. I guess I'll worry about it tomorrow. It's funny, though, Mas—" She stopped.

"What'd you say?!"

"Mason. The way he's a ringleader yet—"

"No! Mace. You said 'mace'!"

Lightbulbs started a riot in front of my eyes like warning signals gone haywire at a train crossing. I leapt up and did a John Travolta in the middle of the office, finger pointed triumphantly skyward. I kissed Luchetti's startled mug and told her what Charley Canton had overheard the night of Kishida's murder.

"Wow," Lydia said appreciatively.

I called the S.F.P.D. Penayo wasn't in, but I spoke with a conscientious underling who listened as a mere dime-store snoop explained that Christopher Mason—and an associate— might have killed Kent Kishida.

I still couldn't grasp the motive. The cop seemed to take me seriously, anyway—he promised the department would check out Mason. He wanted to send a squad car around for me, too, but I told him I'd rather come in tomorrow and speak directly with Inspector Elvia Penayo. Reluctantly, he agreed.

When I said goodbye to Luchetti, she looked up from her makeshift bed, an indefinable expression etched on her face. It was sad and uncertain, transitory, an invitation or a reproach. I was careful to lock the door behind me on the way out.

I left the Schwinn and caught a cab to Hamm's place. He lived over the hill near the fashionable stretch of Polk Street, though his apartment building was a bland cube of concrete and steel carved into studio apartments the size of your average lunchbox. Hamm was young, skinny, and prettier than a Ken doll, with a compelling butch swagger to top it off. He told me he and Kent had been boyfriends for a while, but they got along much better as cruising buddies. His voice got husky when he said that.

I explained that Bartholomew Lane had hired me to investigate Kent's death.

Hamm nodded. "Kishi was fond of Laney. But he wasn't into him . . . that way, you know?"

"Yeah."

He ran a hand through his boyish buzz cut and gave me details about the harassing phone calls. Standard fag-bashing rhetoric, Hamm said. He also told me he knew about the hate mail Kishida had received, and figured the same people were trying to drum him out of the Presidio.

"I know who's behind it," I said.

Hamm's jaw was on the floor. "How come I didn't listen to you earlier?!"

I grinned and boxed him lightly on the arm. "That's what *I* was going to ask."

Trip was acquainted with Stuart Clemens and Dickie, whose last name turned out to be Brut. "Perfect," I said jocularly, though really, it didn't seem very funny. I convinced Hamm to help me blow the whistle on the brutes. Between the two of us, we ought to be able to scrape up enough proof of their guilt. But, I told Trip, I didn't think Dickie and Clemens had killed Kent Kishida.

He brooded while I outlined the rest of the saga.

"That's funny," Hamm said when I finished.

"What?"

"Rory Rafferty went to Memphis today."

"What?!"

"I was doing some work outside DEH today, cutting back some shrubbery. Rafferty was telling a superior she had a family emergency and had to go to Memphis for a couple of days."

"Trip—" I bit my lip, thinking of Rory's file cabinet.

"Ma'am?"

"Do you have keys for the DEH building?"

"Yeah," he said slowly.

"Let's go."

Trip Hamm would have made a terrific cat burglar. First he dressed us in matching sets of army fatigues. Mine were a bit snug through the hips. I managed to close the zipper and sneak a peek in the full-length mirror. Green just wasn't my color.

Hamm spirited me along the cool, dark streets on the back of his motorcycle. I watched the city blocks whiz by, a moving travelogue of sight and sound. We rolled through the Lombard gate with no difficulty and wended our way to the back of the Department of Engineering and Housing. None of the pedestrians on the Presidio grounds gave us more than a passing glance.

Breaking into Rory Rafferty's office was about as trying as licking a postage stamp. I let Hamm root around in her desk while I unlocked the metal storage cabinet. My age—Pinky's age—my shoe size. *Voilà.*

25

I had trouble falling asleep that night, not one of my usual afflictions. I found the elusive bottle of Scotch and tried lulling myself with a glassful. It gave me a headache. I called Phoebe, a much better remedy, but half an hour later my eyes were still popped, staring helplessly into the shadowy void.

I turned on the light and groped the floor. *Neon Rain* was resting comfortably on a cushion of unwashed socks. I read until four in the morning. Only when the book ended was I finally able to fall asleep.

My alarm rang at 6:30 a.m., a cruel reminder of my impending trip to the airport. My eyes were two dry orbs, my hair a tangle of gooey gel. The shower helped. So did a little quality time with the fishes, who flapped their scarlet fins at me as if I were Mary Chapin Carpenter denying them an encore. Afterwards I left a message for Laney, requesting we postpone our planned meeting that day. Then I packed a bag, chose an outfit in various shades of brown, tugged on my turquoise boots, and went downstairs to wait for the Quake City shuttle.

Fortunately, the wild-assed driver was as caffeine-deprived as me. I made him idle the van outside the Valencia Street Cuppa? while I ran in to snare two large coffees to go. We made it to the airport in twelve minutes flat.

The best flight I could get on such short notice routed me through Chicago. I stayed awake the first leg of the trip, reading an assortment of airplane magazines. When I'd ODed on Hillary, Chelsea, and the road to the Super Bowl, I handed the stack of periodicals to the guy beside me, a young pup in a Ball State sweatshirt and a pair of pork-chop sideburns. I stared into the gray-green expanse outside my window and contemplated the task at hand.

Trip Hamm and I had gathered vital information last night in Rory Rafferty's office. For starters, we'd learned that Kent Kishida had been recruited by Rafferty—and a coterie of military officers and National Park Service brass—to infiltrate the Presidio neighborhood watchdog group. The Army and the Park Service wanted the inside scoop on the group's plans and concerns. Apparently, they hoped to diffuse any public opposition during the Presidio's transition phase, especially in regard to the clean-up of toxic waste. According to the paperwork I'd found buried in the back of Rafferty's storage cabinet, Kishida had been promised cash bonuses and speedier job promotion in exchange for periodic verbal reports.

There was no direct mention of Kishida's death, but I found a memo from a Park Service administrator to Rafferty expressing the need to enlist another "confidante."

Based on this information, I wondered if Rafferty and her cohorts might have conspired with Christopher Mason to kill

Kishida. But why? Because Kent had threatened to betray them and expose the extent of the Presidio's toxic-waste problems? I had no proof of that—it was merely a wild guess. And why would Mason be worried about Kent exposing the extent of the Presidio's contamination anyway? He'd more likely approve.

Trip Hamm had made the second telltale discovery. While poking around Rafferty's desk, he unearthed a notepad with a clear impression of ballpoint pen marks on the top sheet. Holding it to the light, we'd been able to discern the words Terra Firma, and a number with a 901 area code. Terra Firma ... T.F. Rafferty's notepad listed the same telephone number as the one on Mason's matchbook, the number connected to Felicitas Moret. Somehow, Rafferty and Mason were linked to the same Memphis source. Coincidence? *Mais non!*

Trip told me he'd heard of Terra Firma.

"Kishi mentioned it," he explained as we stole out of DEH. "I think it's an environmental group or something. He said they were nuts."

"'Nuts'? As in totally committed to their work or hopelessly mired in group process or—"

"I don't know, ma'am," Trip said, kick-starting his bike.

"By the way, is Rory Rafferty a lesbian?" I asked, fully aware of the non sequitur.

"Could be. Kishi seemed to get on with her," he responded. Then he squired me home through the hushed city, stoplights blinking yellow against the fog-drenched sky with the workmanlike pulse of a metronome.

Back on Ramona Avenue, I'd called an insomniac friend in Boston who had an encyclopedic knowledge of extremist groups of all political stripes. Terra Firma, she said, was a new, loosely-affiliated coalition of maverick environmentalists who advocated aggressive direct action.

Not unlike the approach Chistopher Mason had championed at the Edinburgh Castle.

I'd called the airline to book a flight.

Now, as we careened to a stop at O'Hare International Airport, snow wafted in lazy gusts across the tarmac. I waited while the plane shuffled passengers, then watched the flurries swirl with increased ferocity as we ascended once more. From Chicago to Memphis, I read a book I'd snatched at the last minute from my Favorite Lesbian Novels shelf—*The Price of Salt* by Claire Morgan, a.k.a. Patricia Highsmith. I liked it even more than I had the first time around.

The weather in Memphis was a carbon copy of what I'd left back home—gray, drizzly, temperature in the 50s. I picked up a sterile, tomb-like Chevy Cavalier from the rent-a-car folks and steered it into town, relying on a street map open on the seat beside me. My plan was to proceed directly to Felicitas Moret's without passing Go, without collecting two hundred dollars. With DeWayne Miller behind bars and Christopher Mason within easy reach of the S.F.P.D., I wanted to find Rory Rafferty and unravel the rest of the conundrum. If unsuccessful, I could always investigate Terra Firma and its possible ties to NTWA.

Or maybe I'd go belly-up and admit my folly.

The address I'd gleaned from the brewery man put Moret on the northeast side of town. Traffic was a breeze once I bypassed the clog near Elvis Presley Boulevard. I'd been to Memphis once before on a pilgrimage with Pinky, but I didn't remember much of the city's layout. The map was easy to follow, however, and I made it to Moret's street in under twenty minutes.

I sat for a moment in the driver's seat eyeing the modest, one-story house with freshly painted white shutters. The garage door was closed. There was no car in the driveway and no sign of movement behind the windows. My watch read 1:45, which meant it was 3:45 p.m. Memphis time. I stepped onto the pavement and squared my shoulders. Then I strode confidently to the front door and punched the bell. No response.

Damn. I checked the mailbox, a brass receptacle attached to the wall near the front door. It was labeled Moret/Blair. There was a meager stash of mail inside the box, but nothing addressed to Terra Firma. I spent half an hour circling the house and chatting with a next door neighbor who gladly gave me a description of Felicitas—handsome, big-boned French gal who favored overalls and chunky black glasses. She was here attending the Memphis College of Art and rented the small house with a girlfriend. Blair. Cynthea Blair.

I thanked the neighbor and trotted back to the Cavalier. I could either wait here or search elsewhere. I decided on the latter option. But first I scribbled a note for Moret, something ambiguous about a hospital equipment salesman who needed to see her. I hoped it would draw her out. I left the note in her mailbox and retraced my route toward downtown Memphis. The sky was already darkening to a somber wash of orangy-gray. I twiddled the radio knob, found a blues station, and kept the volume low.

DeWayne Miller's business was located on Mulberry Street which, judging from the map, appeared to be not far from the banks of the Mississippi. I was hoping I might find co-workers of Miller's who would be willing to talk. Perhaps Rafferty herself had followed a similar strategy, whatever she was up to.

I deposited the car in the Amtrak lot and cruised one block over to Mulberry Street. I walked past a sign for the National Civil Rights Museum and the Lorraine Motel which— I remembered with a jolt—was the site of Martin Luther King, Jr.'s assassination. Miller's office was a few blocks up, a ground-floor storefront boasting two big window displays of surgical tools and sterling-silver carts. I gave the brass door handle a twist—it was locked. Hmm. I couldn't see past the pegged display boards. When I knocked lightly, nobody appeared.

I knocked harder—still nothing. Rats. I was about to pack it in and go sniff out some Southern barbecue when the office door opened a crack. Then it swung fully inward. A white man with a hooked nose and a shock of carroty hair smiled and said, "Come on in."

I stepped into the dimly lit space and opened my mouth to pose a question. That's when I felt something hard and cylindrical nudge the front of my coat. I gasped and stumbled back but Carrot Head pressed tight against me and whispered, "*Come in*, Ms. Fury." Then he poked me again with the solid rod.

I caught a glimpse of polished black metal kissing fabric. I was no expert on these things, but whatever kind of firepower was aimed at my gut, I knew I didn't stand a chance if I tried to run. Pedestrians strolled on the sidewalk behind me, unaware of the gunman playing havoc with my psyche. I didn't dare risk a scream.

Carrot Head clamped my arm with his free paw and shuttled me all the way inside. I grimaced as he relocked the door and shoved me gracelessly toward a back room. The lights were dim there too but, nevertheless, I could see who else was at the party.

Rory Rafferty and a big-boned gal in overalls were lashed into straight-backed chairs. Christopher Mason stood to one side, limbs loose, eyes wary, balancing a kitchen knife in his hand like it was a piece of Waterford crystal.

26

I've been in jams before, but this was looking like a triple-scoop, double-fudge, extra-whipped-cream-with-a-cherry-on-top kind of jam. Rafferty must have thought so, too, judging from the way her face had frozen into a stiff-jawed mask of terror. Her pale eyes flickered maniacally at the sight of me. I wondered if she still thought I was Susan North, network hack from Century City. For a crazy moment, I wished I *was* Susan North—*she* might have thought to pack a pistol.

Get a grip, Fury. What would I do if I was carrying? Challenge Carrot Head to a duel? In that hypercharged window of time before anyone spoke, I reaffirmed my commitment to a gun-free life. It was a touching spiritual moment.

Then Mason broke the spell. "Fuck," he said.

My sentiment exactly.

Felicitas Moret, meanwhile, radiated hostility rather than fear. She bounced a heel angrily against the tile floor, her swollen pink mouth clamped tight as a canning jar. Behind her art-student getup, she was full-figured, dewy-cheeked, with eyes the color of midnight. And just as cold.

Apparently, Christopher Mason felt compelled to keep up the chitchat. "Tie her up," he intoned to Mr. Carrot Head.

"Hang on," I said in my steadiest voice. "Why don't we do some introductions here? You—"

"Certainly, miss," said Carrot Head, as he steered me toward a third ladder-backed chair. "This here's Rory Rafferty and Fel-*latio* More-ette. He's Butch Cassidy and I'm the Sundance—"

"Cut the crap!" barked Mason. He stormed over, fist tight around the handle of his knife, and shoved me roughly into the chair. Then he whirled and brandished the blade under Carrot Head's nose. "Tie her the fuck up!"

"Chill out, Mase. Jesus."

Good, I thought, keep squabbling. Now how could I ruffle them further? I looked at Rafferty, who seemed to be on the verge of hyperventilation. "Breathe," I mouthed silently. Moret kept her gaze directed front and center.

"You know, DeWayne Miller's in jail," I said casually.

Mason turned and flicked his lank hair. I almost felt nostalgic for our happier times. "Yup, that's a problem," he said. "But it's too late now. You never should have come here." His eyes wandered to a red gas can sitting innocuously in a corner.

Oh, shit.

I took some deep breaths of my own, fighting to keep the panic in check. I plugged on, "Mason, I told the cops about you—how Kent Kishida called your name right before he was killed. It was you and Miller, wasn't it? Well, now they know. So—"

"Do they?" Mason looked almost intrigued.

"Yeah."

He lifted his shoulders in a big, shaggy dog shrug. "They have no evidence. They can't pin down a motive."

"*Chris.*" I snorted. "Miller's gonna roll over. They got him on the Muncie murder, too. He'll need to buy himself a little break."

Flick, flick. Mason's eyes narrowed. Carrot Head had dug up more rope and was lassoing me to the rigid chair back. He suddenly blurted, "Yeah, Mase, what *about* DeWayne—"

"Kevin, shut the fuck up!"

Well well. I'd struck a nerve. I still had no idea what was going on: how Moret was tied to these jokers, what Rafferty was doing in Memphis, who Kevin was. I felt the rope pull tighter, binding my hands and pressing uncomfortably against my chest. Suddenly, I urgently needed a bathroom. Tough luck.

I sighed raggedly. Next to me, Rafferty started crying. Moret said, "*Merde!*" and aimed a wad of spit at Kevin's boots.

Christopher Mason spun on his heels and trooped off disgustedly.

With little ado, Kevin hoisted the gas can and began dousing the room with liquid death. I felt my throat constrict and my bladder release, but that didn't bother me at all. Not compared to the visual image that suddenly rose before me, an image of three human torches, charred beyond recognition, the scattered remains of ash and cinder left to smolder in this nondescript office on this average city block on a dreary day in January.

"Mason!" I screamed.

He turned as I bolted to my feet and tried to charge. The chair tripped me instantly. Still bound, I toppled heavily to the floor, but not before Mason lunged forward to deter me. The tip of his knife blade caught me on the right cheek, just below the frame of my glasses. I felt the warm shock of pain, a jolt, like ice on the belly. I tasted blood and listened as Kevin struck a match. Then the men jogged to the front of the office, tugged open the door, and closed it forcefully behind them.

The smell was the most terrifying thing of all. The room reeked of gas, sulphur, fear. I tried to make eye contact with my companions, but my head was jammed awkwardly against the tiles, mired in a sticky, spreading pool of blood. I saw licks of blue-orange flame rise along one wall. I closed my eyes and tried, without success, to inch forward.

I had no idea how much time passed as the three of us rocked and squirmed in our constraints, struggling to make something happen. Tongues of fire snaked closer. I was afraid the room would blow. Suddenly, a splintering crash exploded from the front of the office and pounding feet headed our way. An angel appeared in the form of a towheaded woman in 501s and a motorcycle jacket. Felicitas Moret wailed, "Cynthea!"

The angel slashed Moret's ropes with a Swiss Army knife. Then the two of them worked frantically on Rafferty and me. I was woozy, afraid I might pass out. When my arms were free, I grabbed the hem of my sweater and pressed it hard against my cheek. "Let's go," I tried to roar, but I think it came out in a whimper.

We made it to the sidewalk of Mulberry Street, where the Memphis twilight offered a splendid embrace of cool, sweet air and the beautiful sight of a limitless, star-sprinkled horizon. People looked at us oddly. But not for long. Behind us, DeWayne Miller's hospital equipment business went up in a raucous blast of smoke and flame, a spiraling inferno that decorated the early evening sky with broad, twisting ribbons of gold.

I collapsed against a brick wall across the street from the wreckage. I gulped air and turned to find my fellow survivors. Rory Rafferty was slouched beside me, trembling violently. But I didn't see the other women.

Then I caught a glimpse of black leather and blond hair. The angel was half a block down the street, gripping Felicitas Moret's hand. The two of them tore pell-mell around a corner, away from the blaze, running exuberantly, madly, as if their lives depended on it.

27

It took twelve stitches to close the cut on my right cheek, a two-inch doozy that would probably heal into a half-moon tipped on its side, a scar-tissue frown. Fortunately, the Memphis hospital accepted my group health insurance plan, or I would have had more than a cut and a few bruises to worry about. A friendly nurse ponied up some painkillers. I was temporarily back in action, ready to figure out what the hell had gone down on Mulberry Street. I was also ravenous.

After a quick scrub-up in the women's room, I wandered downstairs in search of the hospital cafeteria. The boys in blue found me hunkered over a plate of salad, bread, and something that resembled macaroni and cheese. They let me finish, then chauffeured me to headquarters where a squadron of poker-faced detectives waited to hear my story.

Rory Rafferty was there, too, but we were kept separate, as if *we* were guilty of abducting, detaining, and nearly immolating a trio of human beings. I told the cops most of what I surmised, which amounted to this:

Christopher Mason and an accomplice, probably DeWayne Miller, had murdered a man named Kent Kishida back in October in San Francisco. Miller had subsequently killed a private eye, Peko Muncie. I wasn't sure why, but both murders had something to do with the actions of environmentalists who were pressuring officials at the Presidio Army base. Mason and Miller were connected to a coalition called Terra Firma, which was headquartered locally at the home of a French art student named Felicitas Moret, who had fled from the scene at Mulberry Street after the explosion.

I watched six pairs of hooded eyes stare impassively as I recited my increasingly fantastic story. I stopped for a moment, adjusted my glasses. If I was wearing a dress, I would've tried a Sharon Stone, anything to frazzle these immovable lumps of scowling cophood. Hell, I couldn't have pulled it off, anyway.

One of them demanded: "What were you doing in Memphis?"

I'd practically forgotten, but I spun a tale about Terra Firma and my need to speak with Rory Rafferty, a military officer who had flown in the day before. "I still need to talk to her," I added, spying her now-slumping shoulders through a glass partition in the interrogation room door.

"Later!" drilled another public servant, who ordered me to take it from the top, again.

After another fascinating run-through, I told them to call Inspector Elvia Penayo of the S.F.P.D. to coordinate the round-up of prime suspect Christopher Mason. I also described Kevin, although, in my present state of burnout, I could only recall a hook nose and a carroty head. I purposefully neglected to mention the leather-clad angel, who I figured must be Moret's squeeze Cynthea Blair. If Moret and Blair had gone on the lam, I had a hunch their motives were honorable. Or maybe I'd lost too much blood to conjure up my usual cynical suspicions.

My gash was throbbing and my throat raw when they finally let me leave the station. Rory Rafferty was loitering near the main exit, fending off a small mob of reporters and photographers. She no longer seemed imposing. Rather, she appeared frail and shaken. A hangdog expression was plastered on her face like a refrigerator magnet beginning to slip.

I was so tired, I didn't know whether to be angry, grateful, or indignant. When I walked up beside her, members of the Fourth Estate migrated toward me like ants to a crumb. I grabbed Rafferty's elbow and escorted her out the door. "We need to talk," I said bluntly.

A taxicab was waiting at the curb, our own private chariot.

Rafferty had booked a room at the Peabody Hotel and offered to put me up for the night. I wasn't crazy about the idea, but I accepted anyway, for lack of a better deal. We had the cabbie dump us at the Amtrak lot so I could retrieve my rental car. Fifteen minutes later we were sprawled on our separate, surprisingly firm beds, discussing crime and punishment. It was twelve-thirty in the morning.

"So you're not in the television business," Rory said dryly.

I gave her my best aw-shucks grin.

She shook her head ruefully. "I *am* sorry about Kent. Was he a friend of yours, Nell?"

"No-o-o-o." I paused. "What did they tell you about me?"

"Only that you're a private investigator. The police wouldn't elaborate."

"No kidding." I rolled over to give the sore side of my face a rest. "Why don't we trade information? You first."

Rafferty fidgeted. I watched. Eventually, she strung some words together. "Well . . . I was interested in this group, Terra Firma . . . I thought–uh . . ."

"Look, I know Kishida was a mole for you guys. You sicced him on legitimate organizations in order to undercut community opposition to the military's plans. I still don't know why that got him killed–"

"Nell! We were trying to save the Presidio!"

I blinked. "*Save* the Presidio?"

"Yes!" Rafferty sat up and wrung a corner of the sheet in her manicured hands. "It'll be enormously expensive to maintain the property as a national park. Some of the funds have been authorized through Congress, but the Presidio has to get paying tenants, too–organizations willing to lease buildings. Like the Gorbachev Foundation, the University–"

"Yeah, yeah. So?"

"So it's a delicate balance. Both the military and the Park Service know how important it is to dispose of toxic waste responsibly. And we're trying! But if these outside extremists start pointing fingers, our paying tenants might look elsewhere. And Congress might withhold funds, too. The land could end up going to private developers, and the whole city would be plumb out of luck."

"So," I said slowly, "by spying on opposition groups and silencing criticism, you're trying to keep hope alive for the national park?"

"Exactly!"

"Hmmpphhh." I didn't articulate my disgruntlement, but it sounded to me like a parallel of the city's SLAPP strategy. If you clamped down on protest, then tourism and business would continue to thrive . . . threats to public health and safety be damned.

"Okay, Rory. What does Terra Firma have to do with this? Why did you come to Memphis?"

Her pale eyes glistened feverishly. She sighed and said,

"After Kent died, we recruited another young man to take his place. Believe me, we didn't think Kent's murder had anything to do with his covert activities."

I did believe her, on that score anyway.

Rafferty went on, "This other fellow met Christopher Mason, just as Kent had, and was drawn into the inner circle of the group NTWA. You know about them?"

I nodded.

"So after a while–after he'd earned their trust–they told him about Terra Firma, this clandestine, really *radical* group of environmental activists."

She made "radical" sound nasty, like a seamy tale of betrayal or a particularly pungent cheese.

"Yeah?" I prodded.

"Terra Firma, it turns out, was planning an action at the Presidio. They'd found out about these underground storage tanks filled with heating oil. They were going to sabotage one of them–force a fuel leak. Simultaneously, they planned to release methylene chloride into the air!"

"What?!"

"It was a PR stunt. They were going to spill toxins, on purpose, to make the Presidio seem like an incredibly hazardous place. It would have been deadly." Rafferty shuddered.

"No shit." I sat up, fighting back a wave of dizziness. "Your spy told you all this?"

"Our operative, yes."

"Did he have any proof?"

"Mm-hmm. He showed us maps Terra Firma had drawn up. With instructions on how to sabotage the underground tanks."

"And you came to Memphis to talk to Terra Firma?"

"To try and talk them out of it. It's ridiculous. I didn't know at the time they were murderers!"

Rafferty explained that her operative–whose name she

refused to divulge—had given her the address to Felicitas Moret's house, which apparently was the base of operations for Terra Firma. When she got there, Moret was agitated and hostile. Rafferty told her what she knew and how preposterous it was, that there must be another way, it was too deadly. Moret broke into a rage.

In a moment of frenzy, she admitted the planned toxic poisoning of the Presidio, and said Terra Firma believed that drastic, attention-grabbing tactics were called for. She also told Rafferty she had found out about Kent Kishida's murder. Mason and Miller—another foot soldier in the movement—had killed Kishida because he was critical of Terra Firma's strategy and had planned to warn the Army and the San Francisco police. Miller had later killed a private eye who got too pushy in probing the details of Kishida's death. According to Rafferty, Felicitas Moret was traumatized because her colleagues had killed for the cause. She planned to expose them.

". . . at that point," Rafferty continued, "Mason and his henchman showed up at the house, dragged us downtown, and began to grill us. Then *you* knocked on the door and . . . you know the rest."

"Wow," I said. "Good thing I left that note."

"What note?"

"For Felicitas. I guess her housemate—you know, in the motorcycle jacket?—I guess she found it and realized where we were."

Rafferty fell back on the bed with a big whooshing sigh. I pressed my fingers against my temples and tried to think. The whole story seemed unwieldy, impossibly convoluted. But it came down to this: Kent Kishida had not been killed because he was gay, a man of color, or unlucky in love. His conscience simply got the better of him. And he made the fatal mistake of telling Mason and Miller he planned to squeal.

"Jesus," I muttered.

So DeWayne Miller had slipped up and was in custody. But Mason and his new sidekick had fled. So had Moret and Blair. Were there other diehard Terra Firmians running around out there? Would they have the nerve to go ahead with their Presidio action?

We'd already been embroiled in conversation for forty minutes and I still hadn't shared my side of the story with Rafferty. I made short work of it, then threw on some clothes for a visit to the lobby telephones. I told Rory I wanted to let her get some sleep. But really, I didn't want her within earshot.

I called my office in San Francisco. Lydia Luchetti was still awake. In fact, I could hear music in the background and Merle's infectious, throaty laughter.

"Lyd?" I asked.

"Merle and I, we're . . . getting acquainted," she said shyly.

I gave Luchetti a rundown on the Mason-Miller scandal. I figured with that kind of ammunition, the *Chronicle* had to give her the front page.

Then I called Laney. We spoke for some time. After apologizing for skipping out on our meeting, I told him I'd submit a written report in the next few days. Laney seemed to appreciate my efforts, but I felt lousy. Sure, I'd helped flush out the facts about Kent Kishida's murder, but so what?

The work of well-meaning activists would be tarnished by a few bad eggs, the Army would emerge smelling like a rose, and the threat of gay-bashing still affected us all, on the job and off. Besides, Kent and his mother were still dead, the full story of the Japanese internment camps was still suppressed, Family Giant workers were still being laid off, a cure for AIDS had yet to be developed, and Christopher Mason was still on the loose.

Geez, Fury, can't you solve any of the world's problems?!

I hung up and fretted, big-time, then dialed Dawn and Charley's number in San Francisco. Tomorrow was

Thursday—I needed to postpone our date once again. This time Dawn was less understanding. We pushed it forward to Monday, but really, at that point, I couldn't have cared less.

Finally, I called Tammie Rae Tinkers in Nashville.

"Hullo?" she answered sleepily.

"Hiya, Rae."

"Nell!"

"C'est moi."

"You forgot about the time difference," she chided affectionately.

"No I didn't."

"What?"

"I'm just down the road, sweetheart. In Memphis."

"What?!"

Rae agreed to drive to Memphis the next day and meet me at the Peabody, 10 a.m. sharp. We rang off.

Things were beginning to look up.

28

A hazy film of white powder was falling on the streets of Memphis when I stepped outside the Peabody Hotel to keep a lookout for Tammie Rae Tinkers. Snow was rare here, the bellhop told me, as he dragged somebody's Gucci bag through a wet smear on the sidewalk. I smiled and stuck a hand out to feel the tender flakes. I grew up in Cleveland and still missed those delirious days of chest-high drifts and angels in the snow.

Rory Rafferty had caught an early plane to San Francisco. She hugged me goodbye before she left, a rigid shoulder-to-shoulder effort about as gratifying as squeezing a mannequin. Maybe that's how they did it in the military. I told her I'd look her up when I got back to town. I had an idea I wanted to pursue, if I could get Rafferty's go-ahead.

I had plunked down a minor fortune for another night at

the Peabody. Then I'd showered and tried to recreate Merle's slicked-back, sophisticated hairdo. The result? I looked like a drowned rat with a centipede crawling across its cheek. My smile was a winner, though, especially when I tucked my chin and tried to convey mystery, like a has-been celebrity posing for a Gap ad. Fortunately, I'd brought a change of clothes: black jeans, white button-down, and a freshly laundered sweater. I completed the ensemble with my turquoise cowboy boots. Just the thing for a reunion.

Rae came zipping up in her off-white Bronco II at two minutes before ten. When she stepped from the driver's seat, I swear she was moving in slow motion, a bigger-than-life screen idol caught against a backdrop of dirty brick and soft gray sky. Her eyes were a shimmering periwinkle, her hair the inkiest black. My chest constricted as she ran up to greet me and suddenly I recognized the little things: the delicate crinkles around her eyes, the same old shade of lipstick, the mole below her left ear that always made me swoon.

She kissed me and said: "Cool glasses, Fury."

I couldn't stop beaming. I brushed snowflakes off her faux leopardskin collar and suggested we go inside.

Tammie Rae Tinkers and I didn't see much of Memphis that day. First we frolicked around the hotel room practicing moves we'd learned years ago from *The Joy of Lesbian Sex.* Then we collapsed on the bed to give our rug burns a rest. Rae made a fuss over my cut and my banged-up head, then she made another kind of fuss over the rest of my body, the kind of fuss they write sonnets about. Finally, panting and giddy, we decided to venture out for a meal.

We made it as far as the Rendezvous Bar-B-Q across the street. Scarred wooden booths lined the walls, burnished soft with decades of wear. I whipped out my miniature penknife and added my own mark to the tabletop of renegade artwork: a ragged heart shot through with an arrow. Over mammoth plates of pork ribs, hush puppies, and greens, we finally got around to conversation.

"What're you doing here?" Rae asked.

I grinned. "Worshipping you."

"I know that, honey," she drawled. Then she picked up her bottle of Jax and kept an eye on me as she turned it bottoms-up.

"I *wish* that was all. Actually, I came here looking for somebody . . . and I wanted to find out about this group called Terra Firma."

"Terra Firma?"

"Yeah, why, you know 'em?"

Rae licked her forefinger. "Sure. I've done some work with them."

"Really?!"

"What's wrong with that? They're the most powerful environmental group in the state. They're community-based, plus they have ties to more mainstream strategists—the Green Party, lobbyists at the Capital. I think they're branching out to other states now—"

"That's one way to put it."

I chomped on a rib and told Rae about Terra Firma's scheme to unleash toxic chemicals at the Presidio. She shook her head the whole time I was talking.

"Nellie, it just sounds like a couple of crackpots. You know, a few crazy guys trying to gain legitimacy by claiming to be with Terra Firma. Really, the organization is as solid as—" She shrugged. "—it's as solid as its name."

Huh. I'd heard three different accounts of Terra Firma's politics. Obviously, "radical" was a relative concept. I asked, "You ever hear of two Memphis women, Felicitas Moret and Cynthea Blair?"

"No-o-o-o, I don't think so. Why?"

"They're with Terra Firma. And now, well . . ." I paused for a swig of beer. "They seem to have split. But it doesn't really bother me. They were pissed about the Presidio action, anyway."

Rae frowned and said, "Are you worried about that? That someone's going to force a spill at the Presidio?"

"Yeah."

Rae made a respectable dent in her plate while I told her the rest of the story. She reiterated that Christopher Mason and Kevin sounded like a couple of loose cannons. She also tried to convince me the police could take it from here. She was right; my involvement with the Kent Kishida case was technically over. But I wasn't satisfied. And judging how badly the S.F.P.D. had botched the Kishida investigation—and the Army's apparent reticence about cleaning up its messes—I wasn't so sure the situation would just blow over.

"What're you gonna do, Nell?" Rae asked disapprovingly. She had always been irritated by my extralegal activities.

I smiled and devoured my last hush puppy. "I'll tell you about it when it's all over."

Rae just shook her head.

We moved on to other topics, like Rae's job, Pinky's newfound interest in her father, the turnover at the White House. None of these matters made us particularly cheery. I asked Rae if she'd thought about moving back to San Francisco.

She gripped my hand across the sticky table. Her lovely wet eyes bore into mine with the force of a blowtorch. I felt a queasy sensation in my gut, as if these few short years of wanting/not wanting Rae were waging a power struggle in the depths of my soul. I wanted her real badly right then and there she was, about to let me down easy. I looked away and blinked. I didn't think I could stand it.

Rae said: "Yeah, maybe."

"What?!"

"My contract is up in June. I could stay in Nashville, but I think I'm going to interview in the Bay Area, too. I heard about this interesting project in Oakland, and I know they're looking for women engineers–"

I sloppied my elbows with barbecue sauce when I pounced across the table to hug her. Rae smiled, then parted her lips and kissed me slowly, lingeringly, right there in the restaurant. It was a ten on the kiss meter, soft, serious, rooted in memory, drenched with desire.

We had planned an afternoon of dawdling in Memphis: Sun Studios, Mud Island, a stroll along Beale Street. Instead, we hustled directly from the Rendezvous back to the Peabody. My friend the bellhop flashed me a knowing grin as he propped open the lobby door. I didn't stop to return it.

Our hands were still grimy from the rib joint as we tumbled together once more, this time urgently, as if fueled by something rawer than lust. Our coats were woolly lumps on the floor, our clothes an artless jumble of reckless *deshabille*. Rae's eyes were violet, coal, the color of bruises, as turbulent as the Mississippi. When I thrust my hand inside her, she shuddered almost instantly, a rolling cataclysm of heat and abandon. I couldn't keep my mouth away, nor could Rae. She flipped me hard, then trailed her tongue along my spine as if tasting buttermilk, molasses, something basic she'd been craving for eons.

When it was over, I got up to open the curtains. The snowfall had ceased; the sky was opaque, a luscious sweep of pewter gray. Rae stood behind me and touched her lips to the base of my neck. Nothing had been decided. Just then, with the light fading and the promise of a whole evening to dally in, it didn't seem to matter.

29

My flight touched down at 1:14 p.m., San Francisco time. Phoebe Grahame was there to meet me, wearing her aviator's cap and clutching a styrofoam cup of Cuppa? coffee. I groaned.

"What?" Phoebe demanded.

"Nothing." I tugged on her earflaps. "Thanks for coming."

The Cuppa? logo brought it all flooding back—my ongoing obligations, my residual unease, my now-flagging caseload. Phoebe drove me directly to the office in her Barbary Coast cab. On the way, she told me the Memphis conflagration—and its apparent connection to the murders of Kent Kishida and Peko Muncie—had been splashed all over the dailies.

The Sixth U.S. Army at the Presidio was on the alert for mad saboteurs, she explained, while the military elite pledged its commitment to responsible toxic-waste removal. Corporate mouthpieces around the Bay Area had also piped up to defend their companies from charges of environmental negligence. "It sounds like a lot of hot air to me," Phoebe interjected.

"Go on," I coaxed.

She continued her summary. Environmental groups, including the Sierra Club, the North Richmond Clean Air Coalition, and Neighborhood Toxic Waste Alert, had expressed their dismay over the Terra Firma extremists. Meanwhile, Terra Firma itself had issued a statement defending the organization's integrity. According to Phoebe, it was all pretty hard to sort out.

I asked, "Did my name come up?"

She laughed. "Honey, you're a hometown hero."

She pointed to the floor near my feet where two days of newspapers were neatly stacked. I ferreted out the morning rag and found Lydia Luchetti's byline front and center, above the fold. I'd earned just a footnote, actually—a brief mention as the San Francisco private investigator who had first pointed the finger at alleged murderer Christopher Mason. I couldn't believe what I read next: Homicide Inspector Elvia Penayo admitted her department had erred and thanked "members of the homosexual community and other individuals who were vigilant in their concern over the tragic death of Kent Kishida."

The Inspector was singing *mea culpa*. Amazing.

Luchetti had also penned a sidebar about NTWA. The group's first public demonstration was now scheduled to take place outside a chemical corporation in Contra Costa County. Evidently, NTWA wanted to distance itself from the Terra Firma scandal and—at least for the time being—the Presidio. But Luchetti's reporting, with its thinly-veiled editorial slant, gave the organization and its wide-ranging goals a nice little plug.

I found nothing in the paper about the Presidio neighborhood watchdog group. Nor anything about the D.A.'s pending lawsuits. Maybe Peko Muncie's death had thrown a wrench into the works. I'd have to ask Luchetti.

I didn't have to wait long for an explanation. When I got to Taylor Street, I discovered Luchetti had cleared out, but she'd left a lengthy note and a bouquet of irises in a wine bottle. Lavender flowers, pink chaise, green rubber tree, magenta chair—yikes. My office had become a hothouse of sensuosity, a lesbian rainbow room. Whoa, my reputation. My eyes fell on the yellow file cabinet. I shivered involuntarily, and poured myself a splash of Scotch. Then I kicked off my boots, propped my feet on the desk, and leaned back in the swivel chair to read Luchetti's note.

The salient points were as follows: the D.A.'s office had put all SLAPP suits on hold. Luchetti thought it had to do with the potential negative publicity surrounding Muncie's murder if it came out he had been working for them when he was killed—the city didn't want its residents to think it was a close cousin of the CIA. Luchetti spoke with Assistant D.A. Conrad Smith, who denied her allegation, but she was sure he was giving her the run-around. In a fit of pique, D.A. Margaret Halliway had admitted as much.

The *Chronicle* had forbidden Luchetti from writing about the issue, apparently due to an internal conflict of interest. It seemed a few board members were as eager to pursue SLAPP suits as the city itself. Luchetti was livid, and planned to fight it from the inside.

Right on, sister, I said out loud. It was the liquor talking.

I read on. Lydia had found a sublet in the Inner Sunset. She and Meg Halliway weren't speaking anymore. She and Merle, however, were talking a lot. Including pillow talk. Maybe *she'd* find out what Merle really did for a living.

Luchetti, you little devil.

The rest of the note was a gush of thanks for my generosity. She jotted some phone messages, too. One of them stood out from the crowd. The Investigations Bureau of the S.F.P.D., Auto Section.

I punched the number.

"Auto Section."

"This is Nell Fury. I got a message you called."

"Hold on, ma'am."

I rose and shuffled to the window in my stockinged feet. The sun cast a deceptive yellow glow on the gritty Tenderloin streets. I cracked the window and felt a chilly sliver of winter air eke into the overheated room. It was nice. A voice came back on the line.

"Ms. Fury?"

"Um-hmm?"

"Are you the owner of a 1975 Datsun B210?" she asked, then rattled off a license plate number.

I gulped. "Yes."

"That vehicle was found abandoned near the Great Highway. The tow company said you'd been looking for it?"

"Uh, yeah," I said, startled. "It must have been stolen."

"Apparently. We had it towed to the city lot. You'll want to come down and take a look."

"Sure. Does it start?"

"I doubt it, ma'am. Somebody flipped the vehicle and left it on Ocean Beach. Don't get your hopes up."

I rode my bike to the lot. The car was a twisted blob of mud-colored metal and spiderwebbed glass. The passenger side was so mangled I couldn't even rescue any trinkets from the glove compartment. I paid the towing fee and arranged to have the Datsun junked. Then I pedaled home, fed the fish, and prepared a tomato sandwich on sourdough with lots of mayonnaise.

My throat felt dry when I swallowed, but I managed to fight off the frustration. Really, no need to get sentimental.

* * *

Later that night, I reached Rory Rafferty at home. She okayed my plan. The next day I went to see her at the Presidio where she showed me maps and put her approval in writing. Rafferty and I would never agree politically, but we had one thing in common: we both had a simmering beef with Christopher Mason.

The military was keeping a watchful eye on the most severely contaminated sites at the Presidio, while police in two states tried to track down Mason. I had another idea where to find him, and the time and the wherewithal to follow it up. Rafferty agreed to pay me what she'd been forking over for covert surveillance. From now on, she added, she'd make a concerted effort to deal openly with neighbors in the community. In fact, she'd already made plans to meet with the infamous Presidio watchdog group.

I felt lousy about collecting a paycheck from the the U.S. Army, but I convinced myself it was okay under the circumstances. I owed it to Laney, not to mention Kent Kishida. I'd just have to make fast work of the assignment. Also, Elvia Penayo would be steamed when she found out about this. But if I played my cards right, she didn't *have* to find out until the very end. Heck, maybe I'd earn a second apology and a little gold star for my troubles.

My final stage of preparation involved Darnelle Comey, ex-employee of E-Z Investigative Services. At least I thought she was an ex. I found out for sure when I called her from a pay phone on Lombard Street. Yup, she'd left the company and was actively looking for p.i. work.

"Good," I shouted over the din of traffic. "That's why I'm calling."

"What?" said Darnelle.

I raised my voice even further. "*I'm calling to offer you a job.*"

"Really?!"

"*Yeah*," I yelled. "Short-term."

"With a firm?"

"*Noooo*." I laughed. The traffic light turned red, bringing the noise level down to a bearable range, more chainsaw than jackhammer. I knew I had to talk fast. "Darnelle, are you free right now? Wanna meet for a drink?"

"Sure. Whereabouts?"

"Ummm . . ." I sighed and glanced down the gaudy commercial strip of Lombard. I just wasn't in the mood. "Maybe you'll come pick me up," I suggested jauntily. "We can go to The Old Clam House."

"Okay!"

"Thanks, kiddo."

Darnelle was an easy mark. She didn't balk, even when I told her where I was. I rested my elbows on the handlebars, admired my fingerless gloves, and waited patiently for young Darnelle Comey, private eye.

30

I ordered a Bloody Mary and a plate of fried shrimp. Darnelle opted for Anchor Steam. We both tore into the basket of sourdough bread the bartender slapped unceremoniously in front of us. I scattered crumbs and swiveled to check out the bright, well-populated barroom. The Old Clam House has an "only in San Francisco" mix of clientele: longshoremen, secretaries, softball players, traveling salesmen, queens, priests, pols, and p.i.s.

The TV broadcast a football game, the jukebox blared old Rolling Stones, and curlicues of smoke rose up here and there like whimsical, wispy stalagmites. Somehow, it all felt right.

Darnelle inquired about my cut. I winced and told the story one more time.

"*Nell.*" She bathed me with big compassionate eyes. "That must have been so scary!"

I turned my wrist and blew lightly on my fingernails, then polished them on my shirt.

Darnelle socked me on the arm and groaned. "Don't you ever take me seriously?"

"Of course I do, Ms. Comey." I clinked my glass against hers. "That's why I called you."

"Oh," she said, blushing.

Darnelle was wearing a kelly-green sweater with a matching ribbon in her hair and big gold baubles hanging from her earlobes. She looked more like a cheerleader than a professional operative, especially with her cheeks pinkened from praise. It was good. Darnelle had the undercover thing down without even trying.

She asked if Tad Greenblatt was back in town.

"Nope, not until Monday."

"So this job—it's with somebody else?"

"Uh-huh." I waited while the barman slid a mound of jumbo shrimp under my nose. "Yeah, I've got a surveillance job that could last a couple of weeks. I was hoping you'd agree to help me with it, you know, alternate shifts. We'd split the fee. By the time it's over, Greenblatt should be able to take you on—"

"Yeah!" she blurted. "All right."

I grinned, dipped a golden nugget in red sauce, and bit in. "Have a shrimp, Darnelle."

"Okay!"

We chewed and laid out the groundwork.

I figured Christopher Mason for a stubborn son of a gun, but I didn't think he'd be foolish enough to go ahead and sabotage the underground storage tank originally targeted. My hunch was this: he'd lay low and work up a new plan. He and his colleague(s) would choose another vulnerable site at the Presidio or they'd pick some other potentially hazardous location in the Bay Area. That meant an infinite number of possibilities.

Darnelle sighed heavily. Then I told her my suspicion. Her green eyes blinked rapidly, her earrings shone like a pair of radiant suns. I got off track a little, thinking of lizards, deserts, open roads. I downed a vodka-y swallow of Bloody Mary, ran a hand through my blunt hair, and wrapped up the scenario.

Darnelle said: "So it's simple. We just follow Stuart Clemens."

"Uh-huh."

"Stick to him like bees to honey?"

"Ummm . . . like scum to a toilet bowl."

"Gross!"

I chuckled and poked Darnelle in the ribs. "Hey, toughen up."

"Oh, Nell."

When I had visited Stuart Clemens at the Presidio, he had pointed out maps on the makeshift wall of his office. They didn't mean anything to me at the time, but later, after conferring with Rory Rafferty, and seeing the maps her spy had provided, courtesy Terra Firma, I realized they were exact replicas of the detailed maps used by Mason to plot the toxic spill. Or Terra Firma's maps were exact replicas of his. That alone didn't prove Clemens' complicity, but I remembered something I'd overheard on Alcatraz. Clemens told Dickie that Kent Kishida wouldn't have worked out as a stool pigeon. Then he'd mumbled something about a windfall, a perk that made all the aggravation worth his while.

Stuart Clemens was supplying Mason and his pals with confidential data about the Presidio's buildings and grounds. Data necessary to stage a deadly environmental accident. In return, he received a nice tax-free bundle to supplement his middling salary. I was almost sure of it. And the way I had it pegged, Clemens would meet with Mason sometime soon to supply him with information for a new game plan.

"Nell," Darnelle suggested nervously, "what if you're . . . not right?"

I smothered the last shrimp with sauce. "Then we've soaked the U.S. military for absolutely no reason." The final bite was easy going down.

We utilized a bunch of different vehicles to sit on Clemens' tail: Darnelle's wood-paneled station wagon, her boyfriend's Jetta, Phoebe's cranky old Plymouth Duster. On the third day of action, after Darnelle relieved me at noon-time, I paid a visit to a used-car dealer on Van Ness Avenue. I arrived with my entire advance from Rory Rafferty, half of my Cuppa? earnings, plus a piddling insurance settlement. I departed with a navy-blue Mitsubishi pickup truck with a dent in the rear fender and a fake cowskin seat cover in the cab. It was love at first sight.

I should have gone home to rest up for more surveillance, but instead I took a spin all the way down the coast to Paci-fica. I cruised home on the highway, listening to old Nick Lowe and flapping my arm out the window like a crazy kid sprung loose for summer vacation. The pickup looked mighty fine on Ramona Avenue, I thought deliriously, before clam-oring upstairs to collapse on the bed.

For a week and a half, Darnelle Comey and I watched Stuart Clemens go to work, supervise maintenance projects, drive home to a small apartment building north of the Panhandle, and frequent restaurants, the YMCA, the Presidio golf course, and a karaoke bar on Clement Street. That was the worst. Clemens hung out with various co-workers, including Dickie, and a few assorted pals who came to his house or met him at the golf course. So far, no sign of Mason, Kevin, or the women from Memphis.

One day Darnelle trailed him all the way north to Point Reyes, but it dead-ended in another work-related task. Both of us grew intimately acquainted with Presidio roads—we dogged him from Baker Beach to the Nike missile site to the cemetery, the hospital, the reservoir, the Golden Gate Bridge toll plaza, you name it. Driving around in my new Mitsubishi with the January sun filtering through the trees, I became convinced the Presidio would, in fact, make a darn good national park.

Life didn't really let up in the meantime. I continued to overdose on Cuppa? coffee. My wounds healed. My facial scar wouldn't be as cool as the lightning bolt on my shoulder, but it had character. Phoebe flew solo. Johnnie Blue got a small part in a movie with Laurence Fishburne. I got my period.

Later, we were graced with another spell of winter rain. Laney was rushed to the hospital after he developed difficulty breathing. He was okay the next day.

Lydia and Merle were becoming inseparable. The 49ers broke Tad Greenblatt's heart. My date with Charley and Dawn was postponed again. Talk about anticipation. Hope the follow-through would be this good. My brother Harry phoned to tell me his girlfriend was pregnant and they planned to raise the child together. Wow. Now all of us Furys were breeders. Our mom would have been so proud.

On the twelfth day of Clemens-watch, I followed my prey down to Mission Street. The rain had stopped but the sky was still overcast, a drab, brownish-gray afternoon dissolving quickly into night. I stayed close to Clemens as he manuevered the one-way turns amidst a growing clog of rush hour traffic. He pulled up to a meter on Ninth Street. I rounded the corner, idled at a bus stop, and watched him walk unhurriedly into a store called the Guitar Center. His hands were in his pockets, his shoulders hunched.

Huh. Guitars. Maybe he wanted to move beyond karaoke. I decided to hang in the bus zone. Hopefully, a zealous traffic cop wouldn't come along and disturb my excellent vantage point. I propped an elbow on my knee, listened to news on the radio, and kept one eye peeled to the Guitar Center door.

Moments later, I cut the ignition and gawked. A familiar figure was ambling down the Mission street sidewalk.

The man had lank brown hair, a reddish complexion, and a coat the color of martini olives. He also wore silver-rimmed glasses and a black fedora. Heck of a disguise. Before he entered the guitar store, he doffed his hat and flicked his mousy bangs off his forehead. Christopher Mason blew it—he should have gotten a precision haircut.

I bolted from the truck and called Rory Rafferty from a pay phone in the bus shelter. Then I sprinted across the street. Out of the corner of my eye, I saw a traffic cop pounce on the pickup, ticket book in hand. Aw, hell. I slowed my steps and walked nonchalantly into the store. Immediately, a bevy of lads with rock star locks flocked over to greet me. Uh-oh, commission work.

"Hello," I said brightly. "I'm looking for a guy who just came in. Tall, green coat—"

"Oh," smirked a disappointed rock diva. "He's trying out a Gibson. Over there."

He pointed to a glass-fronted booth in the middle of the cavernous store. Mason and Stu Clemens were chatting in the soundproof closet. Mason, indeed, had a guitar slung over his shoulder. He appeared to pluck idly at the strings while Clemens unfolded a rectangle of paper.

I thanked the rock star and moseyed to the booth, pretending to peruse the merchandise. The place ought to be called Guitar Heaven—all the walls, from floor to ceiling, were covered with guitars of every possible hue and design. It was a fantasyland of shiny instruments, the Vegas of guitar show-rooms. I was dazzled by the display, but kept my attention riveted to the soundproof booth. I wanted to keep the men in sight until the city's finest came blasting in.

I made my mistake when I skirted a massive amplifier and tripped over a wire. A cadre of long-tressed fellows jogged over to make sure they wouldn't get sued, and I assured them

I was fine. But the commotion drew Mason's attention. I looked over in time to see him dress me down with hate-filled eyes, then slip something metallic out of his coat pocket. With mounting dread, I watched him jam a handgun against Clemens' neck. I guess he'd changed his weapon of choice. He kicked open the door of the booth.

"Out of my way!" he roared to the assembled crowd of clerks, musicians, and me.

Shit. Clemens looked mighty unhappy, too. He was being pushed and prodded toward the front door, pistol flush against his flesh. I picked up an orange, laminated electric guitar from a stand near my feet. Guitar Center management wouldn't be too happy about this, but I'd worry about that later.

I steadied my breath and crabwalked along behind them, waiting for a break. I held the guitar by its neck. The front door opened. Mason panicked, dropped Clemens' arm, and gripped the gun in two hands, arms rigid, like Harvey Keitel in *Bad Lieutenant*. An innocent guitar shopper with an outdated mohawk and a bullring through his nose bellowed, "What the fuck?!" as Mason spun and aimed at the fellow's heart. This might be my only chance.

I swung the guitar over my head and brought it down hard on Mason's right shoulder. He grunted and rolled to the floor, but failed to lose hold of the pistol. He hunched on his knees and trained the deadly cylinder right at my head. I was staring down an infinite tunnel of gun barrel when the Guitar Center door banged open.

This time, multiple footsteps came pounding into the store. Homicide Inspector Elvia Penayo was at the front of the pack, piece drawn, eyes flashing, mouth set in a furious snarl. She halted, astonished to see me at the sorry end of a gunfight. Time stopped. Mason gulped air, then shifted targets from me to the mohawk man to Penayo herself. The Guitar Center had never been this quiet.

Whatever combination of rage, remorse, and terror transpired in Mason's mind, I'd never know. Suddenly, he lay back on the floor. The cops swooped in. But not before he put the gun to his temple and pulled the trigger.

31

Two Sundays later, I was killing the after-
noon at the Bottom of the Hill club, an aptly-named tavern on
the downslope of Potrero Hill. I was all by myself at a big
circular table, admiring the lead singer of a country-punk
band, the Swingin' Doors. She had a bare midriff, bell-bottom
pants with a certain Partridge Family *je ne sais quoi*, and a
curtain of silky brown hair she kept flinging around like a go-
go dancer from "American Bandstand." She wouldn't meet
my eye, so I started watching the bass player instead, a cool
number with a deadpan expression and a bulging muscle in
her right forearm. I was drinking Red Hook Ale and having an
awfully good time.

It had taken me a while to recover from the scene at the
Guitar Center. I'd accepted a few new cases and tried to steep
myself in work. But even now, after regaining my equilibrium,

I couldn't erase the image of Mason taking a final bow, the smell of gasoline in a backroom in Memphis, and the memory of Carmelinda Kishida and her son Kent, the two players in this tawdry drama I'd never even met. I had even mourned Peko Muncie; nobody deserved what he'd gotten.

Stuart Clemens had been arrested for conspiracy and accepting payoffs. Based on statements from Trip Hamm and me—and the crude piece of hate mail I produced as evidence—Dickie was brought in for assault, larceny, and civil rights violations. Kevin, Mason's carrot-headed accomplice, was apprehended in Texas as he attempted to cross the border into Mexico. And DeWayne Miller was still in custody pending trial, but I heard he wanted to cut a deal and plead guilty for the murders of Muncie and Kishida.

Felicitas Moret and Cynthea Blair hadn't resurfaced, though I received a cryptic postcard from Greece with a scrawled signature and an admonition to "fight the good fight." I kept the postcard to myself.

In a weird way, Mason and Miller got what they wanted, without having to promulgate an eco-tragedy. Because of all the publicity generated by the Guitar Center incident, toxic-waste problems at the Presidio came under intense public scrutiny. Army honchos—including Rory Rafferty—were hauled out on the carpet. Concerned environmentalists, even outspoken Terra Firmians, got a favorable nod. Serita Dodd and other members of Neighborhood Toxic Waste Alert appeared on Oprah, where they slugged it out with scumbags from the Wise Use movement.

Still, I wasn't swept away with optimism. The same week Lydia Luchetti's articles were making waves on the front page, I found a small story buried deep in the regional news section. A sailor in the U.S. Navy was in the midst of a disciplinary hearing for refusing to participate in the shipboard practice of dumping garbage into the ocean. According to the seaman, plastics, oil, raw sewage, and other junk were routinely chucked overboard in violation of international law. For his resistance, the sailor faced years in the stockade and a dishonorable discharge.

I was working myself into a major-league fret when I heard someone call my name over the melodious twang of the Swingin' Doors. I cranked my head. Bartholomew Lane was moving slowly through the bar in my direction. I hustled over to give him a hug. He returned the gesture, followed me to the conference-room sized table, and requested a club soda.

I went to fetch it, trying to squelch the painful hammering that had started up in my chest. Laney appeared shrunken, hollow-eyed, his skin a pasty green. I returned with the drink and gave his bowler hat a playful knock. "Hey, you. Thanks for coming."

"Where're your other friends?" Laney asked.

"They stood me up." It was true—I'd invited the usual suspects, and everyone was otherwise occupied.

"Their loss," he said, and tossed back a swig of soda.

I smiled.

The bass player had exchanged instruments and was heavy into a violin solo, a tender, yearning, and oddly soothing riff that hushed the crowd. "You like the band?" I whispered to Laney.

He shrugged, eyeballed their ragtag attire, and said skeptically, "They're gay?"

I laughed. "Uh-huh. Queer anyway, for the most part."

Laney and I had already discussed the aftermath of the case, but there was one thing I'd never broached. "Mr. Lane," I asked, "did you carry a torch for Kent Kishida?"

The question brought a hint of rose into his sallow cheeks. He chuckled. "Kind of pathetic, huh?"

"What?! No way. It's sweet."

"Nell." Laney shook his head. "Before I hired you, I was so bitter. So crushed. I thought I'd never get over Kent's death. I'm still angry, furious, in fact. . ." He flashed me a devil-may-care grin. "But now I'm ready for some new action."

I pointed to the stage. One of the guitar players was a gangly fellow in a bolo tie and a pearl-buttoned shirt. "How about him?"

"Not my type," Laney groused.

I snorted and drank some beer. The Swingin' Doors picked up the pace. My bell-bottomed friend wailed: ". . .after having lunch with you, I went home, threw myself down and cried. It's *hope*less, baby, I fell for you. . ."

Laney was giving me the once-over. "How about you, my dear? Any heartthrobs?"

I squirmed and felt a funny twinge, as if my throat was bound with lacy gauze. Rae had sent a letter last week—she was coming to town in April to interview for the Oakland job. I said: "A few."

We stayed until the end of the set. Bartholomew Lane was running out of steam and I wanted to stop by Wasteland, a post-grunge/New Romantic clothing emporium on Haight Street. Laney asked why.

"My daughter, Pinky. She got a summer job as a ranch hand at this place in Montana." It wasn't Wyoming, but it was close. "I want to get her something—maybe a suede jacket with fringe, a hat, a vest. Something."

Laney's eyes burned with an indecipherable hunger.

I asked, "Wanna come along? Maybe afterwards we can drive up to Twin Peaks, look around."

"Okay."

I gave Ms. Bell-bottom's exposed midriff one final glance. Outside, the Mitsubishi was collecting winter grime. I unlocked the passenger door, drew a peace sign on the window with my forefinger, then climbed in and turned the key. The truck purred with life.

I flipped a U and motored toward the center of town as a filigree of light broke through the cloud cover like rust slowly rising on a rail.

Spinsters Ink was founded in 1978 to produce vital books for diverse women's communities. In 1986 we merged with Aunt Lute Books to become Spinsters/Aunt Lute. In 1990, the Aunt Lute Foundation became an independent nonprofit publishing program. In 1992, Spinsters moved to Minnesota.

Spinsters Ink is committed to publishing novels and nonfiction works by women that deal with significant issues from a feminist perspective: books that not only name crucial issues in women's lives, but more importantly encourage change and growth; books that help make the best in our lives more possible.